Means of Evil

Means of Evil

Five Mystery Stories by an Edgar Award–Winning Writer

———◆———

RUTH RENDELL

PUBLISHED BY DOUBLEDAY & COMPANY, INC.
GARDEN CITY, NEW YORK
1980

Acknowledgements

"OLD WIVES' TALES" by Ruth Rendell. Originally appeared under the title of "Clutching at Straws" in *Ellery Queen's Mystery Magazine*. Copyright © 1979 by Kingsmarkham Enterprises Ltd. Reprinted by permission of author and arrangement with EQMM.

"ACHILLES HEEL" by Ruth Rendell. Originally appeared under the title of "Inspector Wexford on Holiday" in *Ellery Queen's Mystery Magazine*. Copyright © 1978 by Kingsmarkham Enterprises Ltd. Reprinted by permission of author and arrangement with EQMM.

"WHEN THE WEDDING WAS OVER" by Ruth Rendell. Originally appeared under the title "Inspector Wexford and the Winchurch Affair" in *Ellery Queen's Mystery Magazine*. Copyright © 1979 by Kingsmarkham Enterprises Ltd. Reprinted by permission of author and arrangement with EQMM.

To Jane Bakerman

Contents

Author's Note

Of these five stories three have already appeared in *Ellery Queen's Mystery Magazine*. "Means of Evil" and "Ginger and the Kingsmarkham Chalk Circle" are new and were specially written for this collection.

Each story is a case for Chief Inspector Wexford and each is intended as part of the chronicles of Kingsmarkham. The events related in the personal lives of Wexford and Burden and their families are as "true" as any circumstances in the Wexford novels. The stories should be read as if each were a little novel in the series.

Means of Evil

Means of Evil

"Blewits," said Inspector Burden, "parasols, horns of plenty, morels and boletus. Mean anything to you?"

Chief Inspector Wexford shrugged. "Sounds like one of those magazine quizzes. What have these in common? I'll make a guess and say they're crustacea. Or sea anemones. How about that?"

"They are edible fungi," said Burden.

"Are they now? And what have edible fungi to do with Mrs. Hannah Kingman throwing herself off, or being pushed off, a balcony?"

The two men were sitting in Wexford's office at the police station, Kingsmarkham, in the County of Sussex. The month was November, but Wexford had only just returned from his holiday. And while he had been away, enjoying in Cornwall an end of October that had been more summery than the summer, Hannah Kingman had committed suicide. Or so Burden had thought at first. Now he was in a dilemma, and as soon as Wexford had walked in that Monday morning, Burden had begun to tell the whole story to his chief.

Wexford, getting on for sixty, was a tall, ungainly, rather ugly man who had once been fat to the point of obesity but had slimmed to gauntness for reasons of health. Nearly twenty years his junior, Burden had the slenderness of a man who has always been thin. His face was ascetic, handsome in a frosty way. The older man, who had a good wife who looked after him devotedly, nevertheless always looked as if his clothes came off the peg from the War on Want Shop, while the younger, a widower, was sartorially immaculate. A tramp and a Beau Brummell, they seemed to be, but the dandy relied on the tramp, trusted him, understood his powers and his perception. In secret he almost worshipped him.

Without his chief he had felt a little at sea in this case. Everything had pointed at first to Hannah Kingman's having killed herself. She had been a manic-depressive, with a strong sense of her own inadequacy; apparently her marriage, though not of long duration, had been unhappy, and her previous marriage had failed. Even in the absence of a suicide note or suicide threats, Burden would have taken her death for self-destruction—if her brother hadn't come along and told him about the edible fungi. And Wexford hadn't been there to do what he always could do, sort out sheep from goats and wheat from chaff.

"The thing is," Burden said across the desk, "we're not looking for proof of murder so much as proof of *attempted* murder. Axel Kingman could have pushed his wife off that balcony—he has no alibi for the time in question—but I had no reason to think he had done so until I was told of an attempt to murder her some two weeks before."

"Which attempt has something to do with edible fungi?"

Burden nodded. "Say with administering to her some noxious substance in a stew made from edible fungi. Though if he did it, God knows how he did it, because three other people, including himself, ate the stew without ill effects. I think I'd better tell you about it from the beginning."

"I think you had," said Wexford.

"The facts," Burden began, very like a Prosecuting Counsel, "are as follows. Axel Kingman is thirty-five years old and he keeps a health-food shop here in the High Street called Harvest Home. Know it?" When Wexford signified by a nod that he did, Burden went on, "He used to be a teacher in Myringham, and for about seven years before he came here he'd been living with a woman named Corinne Last. He left her, gave up his job, put all the capital he had into this shop, and married a Mrs. Hannah Nicholson."

"He's some sort of food freak, I take it," said Wexford.

Burden wrinkled his nose. "Lot of affected nonsense," he said. "Have you ever noticed what thin pale weeds these health-food people are? While the folks who live on roast beef and suet and whisky and plum cake are full of beans and rarin' to go."

"Is Kingman a thin pale weed?"

"A feeble—what's the word?—aesthete, if you ask me. Anyway, he and Hannah opened this shop and took a flat in the high-rise tower our planning geniuses have been pleased to raise over the top of it. The fifth floor. Corinne Last, according to her and according to Kingman, accepted the situation after a while and they all remained friends."

"Tell me about them," Wexford said. "Leave the facts for a bit and tell me about them."

Burden never found this easy. He was inclined to describe people as "just ordinary" or "just like anyone else", a negative attitude which exasperated Wexford. So he made an effort. "Kingman looks the sort who wouldn't hurt a fly. The fact is, I'd apply the word gentle to him if

I wasn't coming round to thinking he's a cold-blooded
wife-killer. He's a total abstainer with a bee in his bonnet
about drink. His father went bankrupt and finally died of
alcoholism, and our Kingman is an anti-booze fanatic.

"The dead woman was twenty-nine. Her first husband
left her after six months of marriage and went off with
some girl friend of hers. Hannah went back to live with
her parents and had a part-time job helping with the
meals at the school where Kingman was a teacher. That
was where they met."

"And the other woman?" said Wexford.

Burden's face took on a repressive expression. Sex outside marriage, however sanctioned by custom and general
approval, was always distasteful to him. That, in the
course of his work, he almost daily came across illicit sex
had done nothing to mitigate his disapproval. As Wexford
sometimes derisively put it, you would think that in Burden's eyes all the suffering in the world, and certainly all
the crime, somehow derived from men and women going
to bed together outside the bonds of wedlock. "God
knows why he didn't marry her," Burden now said. "Personally I think things were a lot better in the days when
education authorities put their foot down about immoral-
ity among teachers."

"Let's not have your views on that now, Mike," said
Wexford. "Presumably Hannah Kingman didn't die because her husband didn't come to her a pure virgin."

Burden flushed slightly. "I'll tell you about this Corinne
Last. She's very good-looking, if you like the dark sort of
intense type. Her father left her some money and the
house where she and Kingman lived, and she still lives in
it. She's one of those women who seem to be good at everything they put their hands to. She paints and sells her
paintings. She makes her own clothes, she's more or less

the star in the local dramatic society, she's a violinist and plays in some string trio. Also she writes for health magazines and she's the author of a cookery book."

"It would look then," Wexford put in, "as if Kingman split up with her because all this was more than he could take. And hence he took up with the dull little school-meals lady. No competition from her, I fancy."

"I daresay you're right. As a matter of fact, that theory has already been put to me."

"By whom?" said Wexford. "Just where did you get all this information, Mike?"

"From an angry young man, the fourth member of the quartet, who happens to be Hannah's brother. His name is John Hood and I think he's got a lot more to tell. But it's time I left off describing the people and got on with the story.

"No one saw Hannah fall from the balcony. It happened last Thursday afternoon at about four. According to her husband, he was in a sort of office behind the shop doing what he always did on early-closing day—stock-taking and sticking labels on various bottles and packets.

"She fell onto a hard-top parking area at the back of the flats, and her body was found by a neighbour a couple of hours later between two parked cars. We were sent for, and Kingman seemed to be distraught. I asked him if he had had any idea that his wife might have wished to take her own life and he said she had never threatened to do so but had lately been very depressed and there had been quarrels, principally about money. Her doctor had put her on tranquillizers—of which, by the way, Kingman disapproved—and the doctor himself, old Dr. Castle, told me Mrs. Kingman had been to him for depression and because she felt her life wasn't worth living and she was a drag on her husband. He wasn't surprised that she had killed herself and neither, by that time, was I. We were all set for an inquest verdict of suicide while the balance of the mind was disturbed when John Hood walked in here and told me Kingman had attempted to murder his wife on a previous occasion."

"He told you just like that?"

"Pretty well. It's plain he doesn't like Kingman, and no doubt he was fond of his sister. He also seems to like and admire Corinne Last. He told me that on a Saturday night at the end of October the four of them had a meal together in the Kingmans' flat. It was a lot of vegetarian stuff cooked by Kingman—he always did the cooking—and one of the dishes was made out of what I'm old-fashioned enough, or narrow-minded enough, to call toadstools. They all ate it and they were all OK but for Hannah who got up from the table, vomited for hours, and apparently was quite seriously ill."

Wexford's eyebrows went up. "Elucidate, please," he said.

Burden sat back, put his elbows on the arms of the chair, and pressed the tips of his fingers together. "A few days before this meal was eaten, Kingman and Hood met at the squash club of which they are both members. Kingman told Hood that Corinne Last had promised to get him some edible fungi called shaggy caps from her own garden, the garden of the house which they had at one time shared. A crop of these things show themselves every autumn under a tree in this garden. I've seen them myself, but we'll come to that in a minute.

"Kingman's got a thing about using weeds and whatnot for cooking, makes salads out of dandelion and sorrel, and he swears by this fungi rubbish, says they've got far more flavour than mushrooms. Give me something that comes in a plastic bag from the supermarket every time, but no doubt it takes all sorts to make a world. By the way, this cookbook of Corinne Last's is called *Cooking for Nothing*, and all the recipes are for making dishes out of stuff you pull up by the wayside or pluck from the hedgerow."

"These warty blobs or spotted puffets or whatever, had he cooked them before?"

"Shaggy caps," said Burden, grinning, "or *coprinus comatus*. Oh, yes, every year, and every year he and Corinne had eaten the resulting stew. He told Hood he was going to cook them again this time, and Hood says he seemed very grateful to Corinne for being so—well, magnanimous."

"Yes, I can see it would have been a wrench for her. Like hearing 'our tune' in the company of your ex-lover and your supplanter." Wexford put on a vibrant growl. "'Can you bear the sight of me eating our toadstools with another?'"

"As a matter of fact," said Burden seriously, "it could have been just like that. Anyway, the upshot of it was that Hood was invited round for the following Saturday to taste these delicacies and was told that Corinne would be there. Perhaps it was that fact which made him accept. Well, the day came. Hood looked in on his sister at lunchtime. She showed him the pot containing the stew which Kingman had already made and she said *she had tasted it* and it was delicious. She also showed Hood half a dozen specimens of shaggy caps which she said Kingman hadn't needed and which they would fry for their breakfast. This is what she showed him."

Burden opened a drawer in the desk and produced one of those plastic bags which he had said so inspired him with confidence. But the contents of this one hadn't come from a supermarket. He removed the wire fastener and tipped out four whitish scaly objects. They were egg-shaped, or rather elongated ovals, each with a short fleshy stalk.

"I picked them myself this morning," he said, "from Corinne Last's garden. When they get bigger, the egg-shaped bit opens like an umbrella, or a pagoda really, and there are sort of black gills underneath. You're supposed to eat them when they're in the stage these are."

"I suppose you've got a book on fungi?" said Wexford.

"Here." This also was produced from the drawer. *British Fungi, Edible and Poisonous.* "And here we are—shaggy caps."

Burden had opened it at the *Edible* section and at a line and wash drawing of the species he held in his hand. He passed it to the chief inspector.

"*Coprinus comatus,*" Wexford read aloud, "*a common species, attaining when full-grown a height of nine inches. The fungus is frequently to be found, during late summer and autumn, growing in fields, hedgerows and often in gardens. It should be eaten before the cap opens and disgorges its inky fluid, but is at all times quite harmless.*" He put the book down but didn't close it. "Go on, please, Mike," he said.

"Hood called for Corinne and they arrived together. They got there just after eight. At about eight-fifteen they all sat down to table and began the meal with avocado *vinaigrette.* The next course was to be the stew, followed by nut cutlets with a salad and then an applecake. Very obviously, there was no wine or liquor of any sort on account of Kingman's prejudice. They drank grape juice from the shop.

"The kitchen opens directly out of the living-dining room. Kingman brought in the stew in a large tureen and served it himself at the table, beginning, of course, with Corinne. Each one of those shaggy caps had been sliced in half lengthwise and the pieces were floating in a thickish gravy to which carrots, onions and other vegetables had been added. Now, ever since he had been invited to this meal, Hood had been feeling uneasy about eating fungi, but Corinne had reassured him, and once he began to eat it and saw the others were eating it quite happily, he stopped worrying for the time being. In fact, he had a second helping.

"Kingman took the plates out and the tureen and immediately *rinsed them under the tap*. Both Hood and Corinne Last have told me this, though Kingman says it was something he always did, being fastidious about things of that sort."

"Surely his ex-girl friend could confirm or deny that," Wexford put in, "since they lived together for so long."

"We must ask her. All traces of the stew were rinsed away. Kingman then brought in the nut concoction and the salad, but before he could begin to serve them Hannah jumped up, covered her mouth with her napkin, and rushed to the bathroom.

"After a while Corinne went to her. Hood could hear a violent vomiting from the bathroom. He remained in the living room while Kingman and Corinne were both in the bathroom with Hannah. No one ate any more. Kingman eventually came back, said that Hannah must have picked up some 'bug' and that he had put her to bed. Hood went into the bedroom where Hannah was lying on the bed with Corinne beside her. Hannah's face was greenish and covered with sweat and she was evidently in great pain because while he was there she doubled up and groaned. She had to go to the bathroom again and that time Kingman had to carry her back.

"Hood suggested Dr. Castle should be sent for, but this was strenuously opposed by Kingman who dislikes doc-

tors and is one of those people who go in for herbal
remedies—raspberry leaf tablets and camomile tea and
that sort of thing. Also he told Hood rather absurdly that
Hannah had had quite enough to do with doctors and
that if this wasn't some gastric germ it was the result of
her taking 'dangerous' tranquillizers.

"Hood thought Hannah was seriously ill and the argu-
ment got heated, with Hood trying to make Kingman either call a doctor or take her to a hospital. Kingman
wouldn't and Corinne took his part. Hood is one of those
angry but weak people who are all bluster, and although
he might have called a doctor himself, he didn't. The
effect on him of Corinne again, I suppose. What he did do
was tell Kingman he was a fool to mess about cooking
things everyone knew weren't safe, to which Kingman
replied that if the shaggy caps were dangerous, how was
if they weren't all ill? Eventually, at about midnight,
Hannah stopped retching, seemed to have no more pain,
and fell asleep. Hood drove Corinne home, returned to
the Kingmans' and remained there for the rest of the
night, sleeping on their sofa.

"In the morning Hannah seemed perfectly well, though
weak, which rather upset Kingman's theory about the
gastric bug. Relations between the brothers-in-law were
strained. Kingman said he hadn't liked Hood's suggestions and that when he wanted to see his sister he, Kingman, would rather he came there when he was out or in
the shop. Hood went off home, and since that day he
hasn't seen Kingman.

"The day after his sister's death he stormed in here,
told me what I've told you, and accused Kingman of trying to poison Hannah. He was wild and nearly hysterical,
but I felt I couldn't dismiss this allegation as—well, the
ravings of a bereaved person. There were too many pecul-

iar circumstances, the unhappiness of the marriage, the fact of Kingman rinsing those plates, his refusal to call a doctor. Was I right?"

Burden stopped and sat waiting for approval. It came in the form of a not very enthusiastic nod.

After a moment Wexford spoke. "Could Kingman have pushed her off that balcony, Mike?"

"She was a small fragile woman. It was physically possible. The back of the flats isn't overlooked. There's nothing behind but the parking area and then open fields. Kingman could have gone up by the stairs instead of using the lift and come down by the stairs. Two of the flats on the lower floors are empty. Below the Kingmans lives a bedridden woman whose husband was at work. Below that the tenant, a young married woman, was in but she saw and heard nothing. The invalid says she thinks she heard a scream during the afternoon but she did nothing about it, and if she did hear it, so what? It seems to me that a suicide, in those circumstances, is as likely to cry out as a murder victim."

"OK," said Wexford. "Now to return to the curious business of this meal. The idea would presumably be that Kingman intended to kill her that night but that his plan misfired because whatever he gave her wasn't toxic enough. She was very ill but she didn't die. He chose those means and that company so that he would have witnesses to his innocence. They all ate the stew out of the same tureen, but only Hannah was affected by it. How then are you suggesting he gave her whatever poison he did give her?"

"I'm not," said Burden frankly, "but others are making suggestions. Hood's a bit of a fool, and first of all he would only keep on about all fungi being dangerous and the whole dish being poisonous. When I pointed out that this was obviously not so, he said Kingman must have slipped something into Hannah's plate, or else it was the salt."

"What salt?"

"He remembered that no one but Hannah took salt with the stew. But that's absurd because Kingman couldn't have known that would happen. And, incidentally, to another point we may as well clear up now—the avocados were quite innocuous. Kingman halved them *at the table* and the *vinaigrette* sauce was served in a jug. The bread was not in the form of rolls but a home-made wholemeal loaf. If there was anything there which shouldn't have been it was in the stew all right.

"Corinne Last refuses to consider the possibility that Kingman might be guilty. But when I pressed her she said she was not actually sitting at the table while the stew was served. She had got up and gone into the hall to fetch her handbag. So she didn't see Kingman serve Hannah." Burden reached across and picked up the book Wexford had left open at the description and drawing of the shaggy caps. He flicked over to the *Poisonous* section and pushed the book back to Wexford. "Have a look at some of these."

"Ah, yes," said Wexford. "Our old friend, the fly agaric. A nice-looking little red job with white spots, much favoured by illustrators of children's books. They usually stick a frog on top of it and a gnome underneath. I see that when ingested it causes nausea, vomiting, tetanic convulsions, coma and death. Lots of these agarics, aren't there? Purple, crested, warty, verdigris—all more or less lethal. Aha! The death cap, *amanita phalloides*. How very unpleasant. The most dangerous fungus known, it says here. Very small quantities will cause intense suffering and often death. So where does all that get us?"

"The death cap, according to Corinne Last, is quite common round here. What she doesn't say, but what I infer, is that Kingman could have got hold of it easily. Now suppose he cooked just one specimen separately and dropped it into the stew just before he brought it in from the kitchen? When he comes to serve Hannah he spoons up for her this specimen, or the pieces of it, in the same way as someone might select a special piece of chicken for someone out of a casserole. The gravy was thick, it wasn't like thin soup."

Wexford looked dubious. "Well, we won't dismiss it as a theory. If he had contaminated the rest of the stew and others had been ill, that would have made it look even more like an accident, which was presumably what he wanted. But there's one drawback to that, Mike. If he meant Hannah to die, and was unscrupulous enough not to mind about Corinne and Hood being made ill, why did he rinse the plates? To *prove* that it was an accident, he would have wanted above all to keep some of that stew for analysis when the time came, for analysis would have shown the presence of poisonous as well as non-poisonous fungi, and it would have seemed that he had merely been careless.

"But let's go and talk to these people, shall we?"

The shop called Harvest Home was closed. Wexford and Burden went down an alley at the side of the block, passed the glass-doored main entrance, and went to the back to a door that was labelled *Stairs and Emergency Exit.* They entered a small tiled vestibule and began to mount a steepish flight of stairs.

On each floor was a front door and a door to the lift. There was no one about. If there had been and they had

had no wish to be seen, it would only have been necessary to wait behind the bend in the stairs until whoever it was had got into the lift. The bell by the front door on the fifth floor was marked *A. and H. Kingman.* Wexford rang it.

The man who admitted them was smallish and mild-looking and he looked sad. He showed Wexford the balcony from which his wife had fallen. It was one of two in the flat, the other being larger and extending outside the living-room windows. This one was outside a glazed kitchen door, a place for hanging washing or for gardening of the window-box variety. Herbs grew in pots, and in a long trough there still remained frost-bitten tomato vines. The wall surrounding the balcony was about three feet high, the drop sheer to the hard-top below.

"Were you surprised that your wife committed suicide, Mr. Kingman?" said Wexford.

Kingman didn't answer directly. "My wife set a very low valuation on herself. When we got married I thought she was like me, a simple sort of person who doesn't ask much from life but has quite a capacity for contentment. It wasn't like that. She expected more support and more comfort and encouragement than I could give. That was especially so for the first three months of our marriage. Then she seemed to turn against me. She was very moody, always up and down. My business isn't doing very well and she was spending more money than we could afford. I don't know where all the money was going and we quarrelled about it. Then she'd become depressed and say she was no use to me, she'd be better dead."

He had given, Wexford thought, rather a long explanation for which he hadn't been asked. But it could be that these thoughts, defensive yet self-reproachful, were at the moment uppermost in his mind. "Mr. Kingman," he said, "we have reason to believe, as you know, that foul play may have been involved here. I should like to ask you a few questions about a meal you cooked on October 29th, after which your wife was ill."

"I can guess who's been telling you about that."

Wexford took no notice. "When did Miss Last bring you these—er, shaggy caps?"

"On the evening of the 28th. I made the stew from them in the morning, according to Miss Last's own recipe."

"Was there any other type of fungus in the flat at the time?"

"Mushrooms, probably."

"Did you at any time add any noxious object or substance to that stew, Mr. Kingman?"

Kingman said quietly, wearily, "Of course not. My brother-in-law has a lot of ignorant prejudices. He refuses to understand that that stew, which I have made dozens of times before in exactly the same way, was as wholesome as, say, a chicken casserole. More wholesome, in my view."

"Very well. Nevertheless, your wife was very ill. Why didn't you call a doctor?"

"Because my wife was not 'very' ill. She had pains and diarrhoea, that's all. Perhaps you aren't aware of what the symptoms of fungus poisoning are. The victim doesn't just have pain and sickness. His vision is impaired, he very likely blacks out or has convulsions of the kind associated with tetanus. There was nothing like that with Hannah."

"It was unfortunate that you rinsed those plates. Had you not done so and called a doctor, the remains of that stew would almost certainly have been sent for analysis, and if it was harmless as you say, all this investigation could have been avoided."

"It was harmless," Kingman said stonily.

Out in the car Wexford said, "I'm inclined to believe him, Mike. And unless Hood or Corinne Last has something really positive to tell us, I'd let it rest. Shall we go and see her next?"

———◆———

The cottage Corinne had shared with Axel Kingman was on a lonely stretch of road outside the village of Myfleet. It was a stone cottage with a slate roof, surrounded by a well-tended pretty garden. A green Ford Escort stood on the drive in front of a weatherboard garage. Under a big old apple tree, from which the yellow leaves were falling, the shaggy caps, immediately recognisable, grew in three thick clumps.

She was a tall woman, the owner of this house, with a beautiful, square-jawed, high-cheekboned face and a mass of dark hair. Wexford was at once reminded of the Klimt painting of a languorous red-lipped woman, gold-neckleted, half covered in gold draperies, though Corinne Last wore a sweater and a denim smock. Her voice was low and measured. He had the impression she could never be flustered or caught off her guard.

"You're the author of a cookery book, I believe?" he said.

She made no answer but handed him a paperback which she took down from a bookshelf. *Cooking for Nothing, Dishes from Hedgerow and Pasture* by Corinne Last. He looked through the index and found the recipe he wanted. Opposite it was a coloured photograph of six people eating what looked like brown soup. The recipe included carrots, onions, herbs, cream, and a number of other harmless ingredients. The last lines read: *Stewed shaggy caps are best served piping hot with wholewheat bread. For drinkables, see page 171.* He glanced at page 171, then handed the book to Burden.

"This was the dish Mr. Kingman made that night?"

"Yes." She had a way of leaning back when she spoke and of half lowering her heavy glossy eyelids. It was serpentine and a little repellent. "I picked the shaggy caps myself out of this garden. I don't understand how they could have made Hannah ill, but they must have done because she was fine when we first arrived. She hadn't got any sort of gastric infection, that's nonsense."

Burden put the book aside. "But you were all served stew out of the same tureen."

"I didn't see Axel actually serve Hannah. I was out of the room." The eyelids flickered and almost closed.

"Was it usual for Mr. Kingman to rinse plates as soon as they were removed?"

"Don't ask me." She moved her shoulders. "I don't know. I do know that Hannah was very ill just after eating that stew. Axel doesn't like doctors, of course, and perhaps it would have—well, embarrassed him to call Dr. Castle in the circumstances. Hannah had black spots in front of her eyes, she was getting double vision. I was extremely concerned for her."

"But you didn't take it on yourself to get a doctor, Miss Last? Or even support Mr. Hood in his allegations?"

"Whatever John Hood said, I knew it couldn't be the shaggy caps." There was a note of scorn when she spoke Hood's name. "And I was rather frightened. I couldn't help thinking it would be terrible if Axel got into some sort of trouble, if there was an inquiry or something."

"There's an inquiry now, Miss Last."

"Well, it's different now, isn't it? Hannah's dead. I mean, it's not just suspicion or conjecture any more."

She saw them out and closed the front door before they

had reached the garden gate. Farther along the roadside and under the hedges more shaggy caps could be seen as well as other kinds of fungi Wexford couldn't identify—little mushroom-like things with pinkish gills, a cluster of small yellow umbrellas, and on the trunk of an oak tree, bulbous smoke-coloured swellings that Burden said were oyster mushrooms.

"That woman," said Wexford, "is a mistress of the art-less insinuation. She damned Kingman with almost every word, but she never came out with anything like an accusation." He shook his head. "I suppose Kingman's brother-in-law will be at work?"

"Presumably," said Burden, but John Hood was not at work. He was waiting for them at the police station, fuming at the delay, and threatening "if something wasn't done at once" to take his grievances to the Chief Constable, even to the Home Office.

"Something is being done," said Wexford quietly. "I'm glad you've come here, Mr. Hood. But try to keep calm, will you, please?"

It was apparent to Wexford from the first that John Hood was in a different category of intelligence from that of Kingman and Corinne Last. He was a thick-set man of perhaps no more than twenty-seven or twenty-eight, with bewildered, resentful blue eyes in a puffy flushed face. A man, Wexford thought, who would fling out rash accusations he couldn't substantiate, who would be driven to bombast and bluster in the company of the ex-teacher and that clever subtle woman.

He began to talk now, not wildly, but still without restraint, repeating what he had said to Burden, reiterating, without putting forward any real evidence, that his brother-in-law had meant to kill his sister that night. It was only by luck that she had survived. Kingman was a ruthless man who would have stopped at nothing to be rid of her. He, Hood, would never forgive himself that he hadn't made a stand and called the doctor.

"Yes, yes, Mr. Hood, but what exactly were your sister's symptoms?"

"Vomiting and stomach pains, violent pains," said Hood.

"She complained of nothing else?"

"Wasn't that enough? That's what you get when someone feeds you poisonous rubbish."

Wexford merely raised his eyebrows. Abruptly, he left the events of that evening and said, "What had gone wrong with your sister's marriage?"

Before Hood replied, Wexford could sense he was keeping something back. A wariness came into his eyes and then was gone. "Axel wasn't the right person for her," he began. "She had problems, she needed understanding, she wasn't . . ." His voice trailed away.

"Wasn't what, Mr. Hood? What problems?"

"It's got nothing to do with all this," Hood muttered.

"I'll be the judge of that. You made this accusation, you started this business off. It's not for you now to keep anything back." On a sudden inspiration, Wexford said, "Had these problems anything to do with the money she was spending?"

Hood was silent and sullen. Wexford thought rapidly over the things he had been told—Axel Kingman's fanaticism on one particular subject, Hannah's desperate need of an unspecified kind of support during the early days of her marriage. Later on, her alternating moods, and then the money, the weekly sums of money spent and unaccounted for.

He looked up and said baldly, "Was your sister an alcoholic, Mr. Hood?"

Hood hadn't liked this directness. He flushed and looked affronted. He skirted round a frank answer. Well, yes, she drank. She was at pains to conceal her drinking. It had been going on more or less consistently since her first marriage broke up.

"In fact, she was an alcoholic," said Wexford.

"I suppose so."

"Your brother-in-law didn't know?"

"Good God, no. Axel would have killed her!" He realised what he had said. "Maybe that's why. Maybe he found out."

"I don't think so, Mr. Hood. Now I imagine that in the first few months of her marriage she made an effort to give up drinking. She needed a good deal of support during this time but she couldn't, or wouldn't, tell Mr. Kingman why she needed it. Her efforts failed, and slowly, because she couldn't manage without it, she began drinking again."

"She wasn't as bad as she used to be," Hood said with pathetic eagerness. "And only in the evenings. She told me she never had a drink before six, and after that she'd have a few more, gulping them down on the quiet so Axel wouldn't know."

Burden said suddenly, "Had your sister been drinking that evening?"

"I expect so. She wouldn't have been able to face company, not even just Corinne and me, without a drink."

"Did anyone besides yourself know that your sister drank?"

"My mother did. My mother and I had a sort of pact to keep it dark from everyone so that Axel wouldn't find out." He hesitated and then said rather defiantly, "I did tell Corinne. She's a wonderful person, she's very clever. I was worried about it and I didn't know what to do. She promised she wouldn't tell Axel."

"I see." Wexford had his own reasons for thinking she hadn't done so. Deep in thought, he got up and walked to the other end of the room where he stood gazing out of the window. Burden's continuing questions, Hood's answers, reached him only as a confused murmur of voices. Then he heard Burden say more loudly, "That's all for now, Mr. Hood, unless the chief inspector has anything more to ask you."

"No, no," said Wexford abstractedly, and when Hood had somewhat truculently departed, "Time for lunch. It's past two. Personally, I shall avoid any dish containing fungi, even *psalliota compestris*.

After Burden had looked that one up and identified it as the common mushroom, they lunched and then made a round of such wineshops in Kingsmarkham as were open at that hour. At the Wine Basket they drew a blank, but the assistant in the Vineyard told them that a woman answering Hannah Kingman's description had been a regular customer, and that on the previous Wednesday, the day before her death, she had called in and bought a bottle of Courvoisier Cognac.

"There was no liquor of any kind in Kingman's flat," said Burden. "Might have been an empty bottle in the rubbish, I suppose." He made a rueful face. "We didn't look, didn't think we had any reason to. But she couldn't have drunk a whole bottleful on the Wednesday, could she?"

"Why are you so interested in this drinking business, Mike? You don't seriously see it as a motive for murder, do you? That Kingman killed her because he'd found out, or been told, that she was a secret drinker?"

"It was a means, not a motive," said Burden. "I know

how it was done. I know how Kingman tried to kill her that first time." He grinned. "Makes a change for me to find the answer before you, doesn't it? I'm going to follow in your footsteps and make a mystery of it for the time being, if you don't mind. With your permission we'll go back to the station, pick up those shaggy caps and conduct a little experiment."

———◆———

Michael Burden lived in a neat bungalow in Tabard Road. He had lived there with his wife until her untimely death and continued to live there with his sixteen-year-old daughter, his son being away at university. But that evening Pat Burden was out with her boy friend, and there was a note left for her father on the refrigerator. *Dad, I ate the cold beef from yesterday. Can you open a tin for yourself? Back by 10.30. Love, P.*

Burden read this note several times, his expression of consternation deepening with each perusal. And Wexford could precisely have defined the separate causes which brought that look of weariness into Burden's eyes, that frown, that drooping of the mouth. Because she was motherless his daughter had to eat not only cold but leftover food, she who should be carefree was obliged to worry about her father, loneliness drove her out of her home until the appallingly late hour of half-past ten. It was all nonsense, of course, the Burden children were happy and recovered from their loss, but how to make Burden see it that way? Widowhood was something he dragged about with him like a physical infirmity. He looked up from the note, screwed it up and eyed his surroundings vaguely and with a kind of despair. Wexford knew that look of desolation. He saw it on Burden's face each time he accompanied him home.

It evoked exasperation as well as pity. He wanted to tell Burden—once or twice he had done so—to stop treating John and Pat like retarded paranoiacs, but instead he said lightly, "I read somewhere the other day that it wouldn't do us a scrap of harm if we never ate another hot meal as long as we lived. In fact, the colder and rawer the better."

"You sound like the Axel Kingman brigade," said Burden, rallying and laughing which was what Wexford had meant him to do. "Anyway, I'm glad she didn't cook anything. I shouldn't have been able to eat it and I'd hate her to take it as criticism."

Wexford decided to ignore that one. "While you're deciding just how much I'm to be told about this experiment of yours, d'you mind if I phone my wife?"

"Be my guest."

It was nearly six. Wexford came back to find Burden peeling carrots and onions. The four specimens of *coprinus comatus*, beginning to look a little wizened, lay on a chopping board. On the stove a saucepanful of bone stock was heating up.

"What the hell are you doing?"

"Making shaggy cap stew. My theory is that the stew is harmless when eaten by non-drinkers, and toxic, or toxic to some extent, when taken by those with alcohol in the stomach. How about that? In a minute, when this lot's cooking, I'm going to take a moderate quantity of alcohol, then I'm going to eat the stew. Now say I'm a damned fool if you like."

Wexford shrugged. He grinned. "I'm overcome by so much courage and selfless devotion to the duty you owe the taxpayers. But wait a minute. Are you sure only Hannah had been drinking that night? We know Kingman hadn't. What about the other two?"

"I asked Hood that when you were off in your daydream. He called for Corinne Last at six, at her request. They picked some apples for his mother, then she made him coffee. He did suggest they call in at a pub for a drink on their way to the Kingmans', but apparently she took so long getting ready that they didn't have time."

"OK. Go ahead then. But wouldn't it be easier to call in an expert? There must be such people. Very likely someone holds a chair of fungology or whatever it's called at the University of the South."

"Very likely. We can do that after I've tried it. I want to know for sure *now*. Are you willing too?"

"Certainly not. I'm not your guest to that extent. Since I've told my wife I won't be home for dinner, I'll take it as a kindness if you'll make me some innocent scrambled eggs."

He followed Burden into the living room where the inspector opened a door in the sideboard. "What'll you drink?"

"White wine, if you've got any, or vermouth if you haven't. You know how abstemious I have to be."

Burden poured vermouth and soda. "Ice?"

"No, thanks. What are you going to have? Brandy? That was Hannah Kingman's favourite tipple apparently."

"Haven't got any," said Burden. "It'll have to be whisky. I think we can reckon she had two double brandies before that meal, don't you? I'm not so brave I want to be as ill as she was." He caught Wexford's eye. "You don't think some people could be more sensitive to it than others, do you?"

"Bound to be," said Wexford breezily. "Cheers!"

Burden sipped his heavily watered whisky, then tossed it down. "I'll just have a look at my stew. You sit down. Put the television on."

Wexford obeyed him. The big coloured picture was of a wood in autumn, pale blue sky, golden beech leaves. Then the camera closed in on a cluster of red-and-white-spotted fly agaric. Chuckling, Wexford turned it off as Burden put his head round the door.

"I think it's more or less ready."

"Better have another whisky."

"I suppose I had." Burden came in and re-filled his glass. "That ought to do it."

"What about my eggs?"

"Oh, God, I forgot. I'm not much of a cook, you know. Don't know how women manage to get a whole lot of different things brewing and make them synchronise."

"It is a mystery, isn't it? I'll get myself some bread and cheese, if I may."

The brownish mixture was in a soup bowl. In the gravy floated four shaggy caps, cut lengthwise. Burden finished his whisky at a gulp.

"What was it the Christians in the arena used to say to the Roman Emperor before they went to the lions?"

"*Morituri, te salutamus,*" said Wexford. "'We who are about to die salute thee.'"

"Well . . ." Burden made an effort with the Latin he had culled from his son's homework. "*Moriturus, te saluto.* Would that be right?"

"I daresay. You won't die, though."

Burden made no answer. He picked up his spoon and began to eat. "Can I have some more soda?" said Wexford.

There are perhaps few stabs harder to bear than derision directed at one's heroism. Burden gave him a sour look. "Help yourself. I'm busy."

Wexford did so. "What's it like?" he said.

"All right. It's quite nice, like mushrooms."

Doggedly he ate. He didn't once gag on it. He finished the lot and wiped the bowl round with a piece of bread. Then he sat up, holding himself rather tensely.

"May as well have your telly on now," said Wexford. "Pass the time." He switched it on again. No fly agaric this time, but a dog fox moving across a meadow with Vivaldi playing. "How d'you feel?"

"Fine," said Burden gloomily.

"Cheer up. It may not last."

But it did. After fifteen minutes had passed, Burden still felt perfectly well. He looked bewildered. "I was so damned positive. I *knew* I was going to be retching and vomiting by now. I didn't put the car away because I was certain you'd have to run me down to the hospital."

Wexford only raised his eyebrows.

"You were pretty casual about it, I must say. Didn't say a word to stop me, did you? Didn't it occur to you it might have been a bit awkward for you if anything had happened to me?"

"I knew it wouldn't. I said to get a fungologist." And then Wexford, faced by Burden's aggrieved stare, burst out laughing. "Dear old Mike, you'll have to forgive me. But you know me, d'you honestly think I'd have let you risk your life eating that stuff? I knew you were safe."

"May one ask how?"

"One may. And you'd have known too if you'd bothered to take a proper look at that book of Corinne Last's. Under the recipe for shaggy cap stew it said, 'For drinkables, see page 171.' Well, I looked at page 171, and there Miss Last gave a recipe for cowslip wine and another for sloe gin, both highly intoxicating drinks. Would she have recommended a wine and a spirit to drink with those fungi if there'd been the slightest risk? Not if she wanted to sell her book she wouldn't. Not unless she was risking hundreds of furious letters and expensive lawsuits."

Burden had flushed a little. Then he too began to laugh.

———◄◆►———

After a little while they had coffee.

"A little logical thinking would be in order, I fancy," said Wexford. "You said this morning that we were not so much seeking to prove murder as attempted murder. Axel Kingman could have pushed her off that balcony, but no one saw her fall and no one heard him or anybody else go up to that flat during the afternoon. If, however, an attempt to murder her was made two weeks before, the presumption that she was eventually murdered is enormously strengthened."

Burden said impatiently, "We've been through all that. We know that."

"Wait a minute. The attempt failed. Now just how seriously ill was she? According to Kingman and Hood, she had severe stomach pains and she vomited. By midnight she was peacefully sleeping and by the following day she was all right."

"I don't see where all this is getting us."

"To a point which is very important and which may be the crux of the whole case. You say that Axel Kingman attempted to murder her. In order to do so he must have made very elaborate plans—the arranging of the meal, the inviting of the two witnesses, the ensuring that his wife tasted the stew earlier in the same day, and the preparation for some very nifty sleight of hand at the time the meal was served. Isn't it odd that the actual method used should so signally have failed? That Hannah's *life* never seems to have been in danger? And what if the method had succeeded? At post-mortem some noxious agent would have been found in her body or the effects of such. How could he have hoped to get away with that since, as we know, neither of his witnesses actually watched him serve Hannah and one of them was even out of the room?

"So what I am postulating is that no one attempted to murder her, but someone *attempted* to make her ill so that, taken in conjunction with the sinister reputation of non-mushroom fungi and Hood's admitted suspicion of them, taken in conjunction with the known unhappiness of the marriage, *it would look as if there had been a murder attempt.*"

Burden stared at him. "Kingman would never have done that. He would either have wanted his attempt to succeed or not to have looked like an attempt at all."

"Exactly. And where does that get us?"

Instead of answering him, Burden said on a note of triumph, his humiliation still rankling, "You're wrong about one thing. She *was* seriously ill, she didn't just have nausea and vomiting. Kingman and Hood may not have mentioned it, but Corinne Last said she had double vision and black spots before her eyes and . . ." His voice faltered. "My God, you mean . . . ?"

Wexford nodded. "Corinne Last only of the three says she had those symptoms. Only Corinne Last is in a position to say, because she lived with him, if Kingman was in the habit of rinsing plates as soon as he removed them from the table. What does she say? That she doesn't know. Isn't that rather odd? Isn't it rather odd too that she chose that precise moment to leave the table and go out into the hall for her handbag?

"She knew that Hannah drank because Hood had told her so. On the evening that meal was eaten you say Hood called for her at her own request. Why? She has her own car, and I don't for a moment believe that a woman like her would feel anything much but contempt for Hood."

"She told him there was something wrong with the car."

"She asked him to come at six, although they were not due at the Kingmans' till eight. She gave him *coffee.* A funny thing to drink at that hour, wasn't it, and before a meal? So what happens when he suggests calling in at a pub on the way? She doesn't say no or say it isn't a good idea to drink and drive. She takes so long getting ready that they don't have time.

"She didn't want Hood to drink any alcohol, Mike, and she was determined to prevent it. She, of course, would take no alcohol and she knew Kingman never drank. But she also knew Hannah's habit of having her first drink of the day at about six.

"Now look at her motive, far stronger than Kingman's. She strikes me as a violent, passionate and determined woman. Hannah had taken Kingman away from her. Kingman had rejected her. Why not revenge herself on both of them by killing Hannah and seeing to it that Kingman was convicted of the crime? If she simply killed Hannah, she had no way of ensuring that Kingman would come under suspicion. But if she made it look as if he had previously attempted her life, the case against him would become very strong indeed.

"Where was she last Thursday afternoon? She could just as easily have gone up those stairs as Kingman could. Hannah would have admitted her to the flat. If she, known to be interested in gardening, had suggested that Hannah take her on to that balcony and show her the pot herbs, Hannah would willingly have done so. And then we have the mystery of the missing brandy bottle with some of its contents surely remaining. If Kingman had killed her, he would have left that there as it would greatly have strengthened the case for suicide. Imagine how he might have used it. "Heavy drinking made my wife ill that night. She knew I had lost respect for her because of her drinking. She killed herself because her mind was unbalanced by drink.

"Corinne Last took that bottle away because she didn't want it known that Hannah drank, and she was banking on Hood's keeping it dark from us just as he had kept it from so many people in the past. And she didn't want it known because the fake murder attempt that *she* staged depended on her victim having alcohol present in her body."

Burden sighed, poured the last dregs of coffee into Wexford's cup. "But we tried that out," he said. "Or I tried it out, and it doesn't work. You knew it wouldn't work from her book. True, she brought the shaggy caps from her own garden, but she couldn't have mixed up poisonous fungi with them because Axel Kingman would have realised at once. Or if he hadn't, they'd all have been ill, alcohol or no alcohol. She was never alone with Hannah before the meal, and while the stew was served she was out of the room."

"I know. But we'll see her in the morning and ask her a few more questions." Wexford hesitated, then quoted softly, " 'Out of good still to find some means of evil.' "

"What?"

"That's what she did, isn't it? It was good for everyone but Hannah, you look as if it's done you a power of good, but it was evil for Hannah. I'm off now, Mike, it's been a long day. Don't forget to put your car away. You won't be making any emergency trips to hospital tonight."

They were unable to puncture her self-possession. The languorous Klimt face was carefully painted this morning, and she was dressed as befitted the violinist or the actress or the author. She had been forewarned of their coming and the gardener image had been laid aside. Her long smooth hands looked as if they had never touched the earth or pulled up a weed.

Where had she been on the afternoon of Hannah Kingman's death? Her thick shapely eyebrows went up. At home, indoors, painting. Alone?

"Painters don't work with an audience," she said rather insolently, and she leaned back, dropping her eyelids in that way of hers. She lit a cigarette and flicked her fingers at Burden for an ashtray as if he were a waiter.

Wexford said, "On Saturday, October 29th, Miss Last, I believe you had something wrong with your car?"

She nodded lazily.

In asking what was wrong with it, he thought he might catch her. He didn't.

"The glass in the offside front headlight was broken while the car was parked," she said, and although he thought how easily she could have broken that glass herself, he could hardly say so. In the same smooth voice she added, "Would you like to see the bill I had from the garage for repairing it?"

"That won't be necessary." She wouldn't have offered to show it to him if she hadn't possessed it. "You asked Mr. Hood to call for you here at six, I understand."

"Yes. He's not my idea of the best company in the world, but I'd promised him some apples for his mother and we had to pick them before it got dark."

"You gave him coffee but had no alcohol. You had no drinks on the way to Mr. and Mrs. Kingman's flat. Weren't you a little disconcerted at the idea of going out to dinner at a place where there wouldn't even be a glass of wine?"

"I was used to Mr. Kingman's ways." But not so used, thought Wexford, that you can tell me whether it was normal or abnormal for him to have rinsed those plates. Her mouth curled, betraying her a little. "It didn't bother me, I'm not a slave to liquor."

"I should like to return to these shaggy caps. You picked them from here on October 28th and took them to Mr. Kingman that evening. I think you said that?"

"I did. I picked them from this garden."

She enunciated the words precisely, her eyes wide open and gazing sincerely at him. The words, or perhaps her unusual straightforwardness, stirred in him the glimmer of an idea. But if she had said nothing more, that idea might have died as quickly as it had been born.

"If you want to have them analysed or examined or whatever, you're getting a bit late. Their season's practically over." She looked at Burden and gave him a gracious smile. "But you took the last of them yesterday, didn't you? So that's all right."

Wexford, of course, said nothing about Burden's experiment. "We'll have a look in your garden, if you don't mind."

She didn't seem to mind, but she had been wrong. Most of the fungi had grown into black-gilled pagodas in the twenty-four hours that had elapsed. Two new ones, however, had thrust their white oval caps up through the wet grass. Wexford picked them, and still she didn't seem to mind. Why, then, had she appeared to want their season to be over? He thanked her and she went back into the cottage. The door closed. Wexford and Burden walked out into the road.

The fungus season was far from over. From the abundant array by the roadside it looked as if the season would last weeks longer. Shaggy caps were everywhere, some of them smaller and greyer than the clump that grew out of Corinne Last's well-fed lawn. There were green and purple agarics, horn-shaped toadstools, and tiny mushrooms growing in fairy rings.

"She doesn't exactly mind our having them analysed," Wexford said thoughtfully, "but it seems she'd prefer the analysis to be done on the ones you picked yesterday than on those I picked today. Can that be so or am I just imagining it?"

"If you're imagining it, I'm imagining it too. But it's no good, that line of reasoning. We know they're not potentiated—or whatever the word is—by alcohol."

"I shall pick some more all the same," said Wexford. "Haven't got a paper bag, have you?"

"I've got a clean handkerchief. Will that do?"

"Have to," said Wexford who never had a clean one. He picked a dozen more young shaggy caps, big and small, white and grey, immature and fully grown. They got back into the car and Wexford told the driver to stop at the public library. He went in and emerged a few minutes later with three books under his arm.

"When we get back," he said to Burden, "I want you to get on to the university and see what they can offer us in the way of an expert in fungilogy."

He closeted himself in his office with the three books and a pot of coffee. When it was nearly lunchtime, Burden knocked on the door.

"Come in," said Wexford. "How did you get on?"

"It's not fungologist or fungilogist," said Burden with triumphant severity. "It's *mycologist* and they don't have one. But there's a man on the faculty who's a toxicologist and who's just published one of those popular science books. This one's about poisoning by wild plants and fungi."

Wexford grinned. "What's it called? *Killing for Nothing?* He sounds as if he'd do fine."

"I said we'd see him at six. Let's hope something will come of it."

"No doubt it will." Wexford slammed shut the thickest of his books. "We need confirmation," he said, "but I've found the answer."

"For God's sake! Why didn't you say?"

"You didn't ask. Sit down." Wexford motioned him to the chair on the other side of the desk. "I said you'd done your homework, Mike, and so you had, only your text-book wasn't quite comprehensive enough. It's got a section on edible fungi and a section on poisonous fungi—*but nothing in between.* What I mean by that is, there's nothing in your book about fungi which aren't wholesome yet don't cause death or intense suffering. There's nothing about the kind that can make people ill in certain circumstances."

"But we know they ate shaggy caps," Burden protested. "And if by 'circumstances' you mean the intake of alcohol, we know shaggy caps aren't affected by alcohol."

"Mike," said Wexford quietly, "*do* we know they ate shaggy caps?" He spread out on the desk the haul he had made from the roadside and from Corinne Last's garden. "Look closely at these, will you?"

Quite bewildered now, Burden looked at and fingered the dozen or so specimens of fungi. "What am I to look *for?*"

"Differences," said Wexford laconically.

"Some of them are smaller than the others, and the smaller ones are greyish. Is that what you mean? But, look here, think of the differences between mushrooms. You get big flat ones and small button ones and . . ."

"Nevertheless, in this case it is that small difference that makes all the difference." Wexford sorted the fungi into two groups. "All the small greyer ones," he said, "came from the roadside. Some of the larger whiter ones came from Corinne Last's garden and some from the roadside."

He picked up between forefinger and thumb a specimen of the former. "This isn't a shaggy cap, it's an ink cap. Now listen." The thick book fell open where he had placed a marker. Slowly and clearly he read: *"The ink cap,* coprinus atramentarius, *is not to be confused with the shaggy cap,* coprinus comatus. *It is smaller and greyer in colour, but otherwise the resemblance between them is strong. While* coprinus atramentarius *is usually harmless when cooked, it contains, however, a chemical similar to the active principle in* Antabuse, *a drug used in the treatment of alcoholics, and if eaten in conjunction with alcohol will cause nausea and vomiting."*

"We'll never prove it."

"I don't know about that," said Wexford. "We can begin by concentrating on the one lie we know Corinne Last told when she said she picked the fungi she gave Axel Kingman *from her own garden."*

Old Wives' Tales

They looked shocked and affronted and somehow ashamed. Above all, they looked old. Wexford thought that in the nature of things a woman of seventy ought to be an orphan, ought to have been an orphan for twenty years. This one had been an orphan for scarcely twenty days. Her husband, sitting opposite her, pulling his wispy moustache, slowly and mechanically shaking his head, seemed older than she, perhaps not so many years the junior of his late mother-in-law. He wore a brown cardigan with a small neat darn at one elbow and sheepskin slippers, and when he spoke he snuffled. His wife kept saying she couldn't believe her ears, she couldn't believe it, why were people so wicked? Wexford didn't answer that. He couldn't, though he had often wondered himself.

"My mother died of a stroke," Mrs. Betts said tremulously. "It was on the death certificate, Dr. Moss put it on the death certificate."

Betts snuffled and wheezed. He reminded Wexford of an aged rabbit, a rabbit with myxomatosis perhaps. It was partly the effect of the brown woolly cardigan and the furry slippers, and partly the moustache and the unshaven bristly chin. "She was ninety-two," Betts said in his thick catarrhal voice. "*Ninety-two.* I reckon you lot must have got bats in the belfry."

"I mean," said Mrs. Betts, "are you saying Dr. Moss was telling untruths? A doctor?"

"Why don't you ask him? We're only ordinary people, the wife and me, we're not educated. Doctor said a cerebral haemorrhage," Betts stumbled a little over the words, "and in plain language that's a stroke. That's what he said. Are you saying me or the wife gave Mother a stroke? Are you saying that?"

"I'm making no allegations, Mr. Betts." Wexford felt uncomfortable, wished himself anywhere but in this newly decorated, paint-smartened house. "I am merely making enquiries which information received obliges me to do."

"Gossip," said Mrs. Betts bitterly. "This street's a hotbed of gossip. Pity they've nothing better to do. Oh, I know what they're saying. Half of them turn up their noses and look the other way when I pass them. All except Elsie Parrish, and that goes without saying."

"She's been a brick," said her husband. "A real brick is Elsie." He stared at Wexford with a kind of timid outrage. "Haven't you folk got nothing better to do than listen to a bunch of old hens? What about the real crime? What about the muggings and the break-ins?"

Wexford sighed. But he went on doggedly questioning, remembering what the nurse had said, what Dr. Moss had said, keeping in the forefront of his mind that motive which was so much more than merely wanting an aged parent out of the way. If he hadn't been a policeman with a profound respect for the law and for human life, he might have felt that these two, or one of them, had been provoked beyond bearing to do murder.

One of them? Or both? Or neither? Ivy Wrangton had either died an unnatural death or else there had been a series of coincidences and unexplained contingencies which were nothing short of incredible.

It was the nurse who had started it, coming to him three days before. Sergeant Martin brought her to him because what she alleged was so serious. Wexford knew her by sight, had seen her making her calls, and had sometimes wondered how district nurses could endure their jobs, the unremitting daily toil, the poor pay, the unsavoury tasks. Perhaps she felt the same about his. She was a fair, pretty woman, about thirty-five, overweight, with big red hands, who always looked tired. She looked tired now, though she hadn't long been back from two weeks' holiday. She was in her summer uniform, blue and white print dress, white apron, dark cardigan, small round hat and the stout shoes that served for summer and winter alike. Nurse Radcliffe. Judith Radcliffe.

"Mr. Wexford?" she said. "Chief Inspector Wexford? Yes. I believe I used to look in on your daughter after she'd had a baby. I was doing my midwifery then. I can't remember her name but the baby was Benjamin."

Wexford smiled and told her his daughter's name and wondered, looking at the bland faded blue eyes and the stolid set of the neck and shoulders, just how intelligent this woman was, how perceptive and how truthful. He pulled up one of the little yellow chairs for her. His office was cheerful and sunny-looking even when the sun wasn't shining, not much like a police station.

"Please sit down, Nurse Radcliffe," he said. "Sergeant Martin's given me some idea what you've come about."

"I feel rather awful. You may think I'm making a mountain out of a molehill."

"I shouldn't worry about that. If I do I'll tell you so and we'll forget it. No one else will know of it, it'll be between us and these four walls."

At that she gave a short laugh. "Oh, dear, I'm afraid it's gone *much* further than that already. I've three patients in Castle Road and each one of them mentioned it to me. That's what Castle Road gossip is at the moment, poor old Mrs. Wrangton's death. And I just thought—well, you can't have that much smoke without fire, can you?"

Mountains and molehills, Wexford thought, smoke and fire. This promised to be a real volcano. He said firmly, "I think you'd better tell me all about it."

She was rather pathetic. "It's best you hear it from someone *professional*." She planted her feet rather wide apart in front of her and leant forward, her hands on her knees. "Mrs. Wrangton was a very old woman. She was ninety-two. But allowing for her age, she was as fit as a fiddle, thin, strong, continent, her heart as sound as a bell. The day she died was the day I went away on holiday, but I was in there the day before to give her her bath—I did that once a week, she couldn't get in and out of the bath on her own—and I remember thinking she was fitter than I'd seen her for months. You could have knocked me down with a feather when I came back from holiday and heard she'd had a stroke the next day."

"When did you come back, Nurse Radcliffe?"

"Last Friday, Friday the 16th. Well, it's Thursday now and I was back on my district on Monday and the first thing I heard was that Mrs. Wrangton was dead and suggestions she'd been—well, helped on her way." She paused, worked something out on her fingers. "I went away June 2nd, that was the day she died, and the funeral was June 7th."

"Funeral?"

"Well, cremation," said Nurse Radcliffe, glancing up as Wexford sighed. "Dr. Moss attended Mrs. Wrangton. She was really Dr. Crocker's patient, but he was on holiday too, like me. Look, Mr. Wexford, I don't know the details of what happened that day, June 2nd, not first-hand, only what the Castle Road ladies say. D'you want to hear that?"

"You haven't yet told me what she died of."

"A stroke—according to Dr. Moss."

"I'm not at all sure," said Wexford dryly, "how one sets about giving someone a stroke. Would you give them a bad fright or push an empty hypodermic into them or get them into a rage or what?"

"I really don't know." Nurse Radcliffe looked a little put out and as if she would like to say, had she dared, that to find this out was Wexford's job, not hers. She veered away from the actual death. "Mrs. Wrangton and her daughter—that's Mrs. Betts, Mrs. Doreen Betts—they hated each other, they were cat and dog. And I don't think Mr. Betts had spoken to Mrs. Wrangton for a year or more. Considering the house was Mrs. Wrangton's and every stick of furniture in it belonged to her, I used to think they were very ungrateful. I never liked the way Mrs. Betts spoke about her mother, let alone the way she spoke *to* her, but I couldn't say a word. Mr. Betts is retired now but he only had a very ordinary sort of job in the Post Office and they lived rent-free in Mrs. Wrangton's home. It's a nice house, you know, late Victorian, and they built to last in those days. I used to think it badly needed doing up and it was a pity Mr. Betts couldn't get down to a bit of painting, when Mrs. Wrangton said to me she was having decorators in, having the whole house done up inside and out . . ."

Wexford cut short the flow of what seemed like irrelevancies. "Why were the Bettses and Mrs. Wrangton on such bad terms?"

The look he got implied that seldom had Nurse Radcliffe come across such depths of naivety. "It's a sad fact, Mr. Wexford, that people can outstay their welcome in this world. To put it bluntly, Mr. and Mrs. Betts couldn't wait for something to happen to Mrs. Wrangton." Her voice lingered over the euphemism. "They hadn't been married all that long, you know," she said surprisingly. "Only five or six years. Mrs. Betts was just a spinster before that, living at home with Mother. Mr. Betts was a widower that she met at the Over-Sixties Club. Mrs. Wrangton used to say she could have done better for herself—seems funny to say that about a woman of her age, doesn't it?—and that Mr. Betts was only after the house and her money."

"You mean she said it to you?"

"Well, not just to me, to anybody," said Nurse Radcliffe, unconsciously blackening the dead woman to whom she showed such conscious bias. "She really felt it. I think she bitterly resented having him in the house."

Wexford moved a little impatiently in his chair. "If we were to investigate every death just because the victim happened to be on bad terms with his or her relations . . ."

"Oh, no, no, it's not just that, not at all. Mrs. Betts sent for Dr. Moss on May 23rd, just four days after Dr. Crocker went away. Why did she? There wasn't anything wrong with Mrs. Wrangton. I was getting her dressed after her bath and I was amazed to see Dr. Moss. Mrs. Wrangton said, I don't know what you're doing here, I never asked my daughter to send for you. Just because I overslept a bit this morning, she said. She was so proud of her good health, poor dear, never had an illness in her long life but the once and that was more an allergy than an illness. I can tell you why he was sent for, Mr. Wexford. So that *when Mrs. Wrangton died* he'd be within his rights signing the death certificate. He wasn't her doctor, you see, but it'd be all right if he'd attended her within the past two weeks, that's the law. They're all saying Mrs. Betts waited for Dr. Crocker to go away, she knew he'd never have just accepted her mother's death like that. He'd have asked for a post-mortem and then the 'fat would have been in the fire." Nurse Radcliffe didn't specify how, and Wexford thought better of interrupting her again. "The last time I saw Mrs. Wrangton," she went on, "was on June 1st. I had a word with the painter as I was going out. There were two of them but this was a young boy, about twenty. I asked him when they expected to finish, and he said, sooner than they thought, next week, because Mrs. Betts had told them just to finish the kitchen and the outside and then to leave it. I thought it was funny at the time, Mrs. Wrangton hadn't said a word to me about it. In fact, what she'd said was, wouldn't it be nice when the bathroom walls were all tiled and I wouldn't have to worry about splashing when I bathed her.

"Mr. Wexford, it's possible Mrs. Betts stopped that work because she knew her mother was going to die the next day. She personally didn't want the whole house redecorated and she didn't want to have to pay for it out of the money her mother left her."

"Was there much money?" Wexford asked.

"I'd guess a few thousands in the bank, maybe three or four, and there was the house, wasn't there? I know she'd made a will, I witnessed it. I and Dr. Crocker. In the presence," said Nurse Radcliffe sententiously, "of the legatee and of each other, which is the law. But naturally I didn't see what its *provisions* were. Mrs. Wrangton did tell me the house was to go to Mrs. Betts and there was a little something for her friend Elsie Parrish. Beyond that, I couldn't tell you. Mind you, Mrs. Parrish won't have it that there could have been foul play. I met her in Castle

Road and she said, wasn't it wicked the things people were saying?"

"Who is Elsie Parrish?"

"A very nice old friend of Mrs. Wrangton's. Nearly eighty but as spry as a cricket. And that brings me to the worst thing. June 2nd, that Friday afternoon, Mr. and Mrs. Betts went off to a whist drive. Mrs. Parrish knew they were going. Mrs. Betts had promised to knock on her door before they went so that she could come round and sit with Mrs. Wrangton. She sometimes did that. It wasn't right to leave her alone, not at her age. Well, Mrs. Parrish waited in and Mrs. Betts never came, so naturally she thought the Bettses had changed their minds and hadn't gone out. But they had. They deliberately didn't call to fetch Mrs. Parrish. They left Mrs. Wrangton all alone but for that young boy painter, and they'd never done such a thing before, not once."

Wexford digested all this in silence, not liking it but not really seeing it as a possible murder case. Nurse Radcliffe seemed to have dried up. She slackened back in the chair with a sigh.

"You mentioned an allergy . . . ?"

"Oh, my goodness, that was about fifty years ago! Only some kind of hay fever, I think. There's asthma in the family. Mrs. Betts's brother had asthma all his life, and Mrs. Betts gets urticaria—nettle rash, that is. They're all connected, you know."

He nodded. He had the impression she had a bombshell yet to explode, or that the volcano was about to erupt. "If they weren't there," he said, "how could either of them possibly have hastened Mrs. Wrangton's end?"

"They'd been back two hours before she died. When

they came back she was in a coma, and they waited *one hour and twenty minutes* before they phoned Dr. Moss."

———————◄—◆—►———————

"Would you have signed that death certificate, Len?" said Wexford to Dr. Crocker. They were in the purpose-built bungalow that housed two consulting rooms and a waiting room. Dr. Crocker's evening surgery was over, the last patient packed off with reassurance and a prescription. Crocker gave Wexford rather a defiant look.

"Of course I would. Why not? Mrs. Wrangton was ninety-two. It's ridiculous of Radcliffe to say she didn't expect her to die. You expect everyone of ninety-two to die and pretty soon. I hope nobody's casting any aspersions on my extremely able partner."

"I'm not," said Wexford. "There's nothing I'd like more than for this to turn out a lot of hot air. But I do have to ask you, don't I? I do have to ask Jim Moss."

Dr. Crocker looked a little mollified. He and the chief inspector were lifelong friends, they had been at school together, had lived most of their lives in Kingmarkham where Crocker had his practice and Wexford was head of the CID. But for a medical practitioner, no amount of friendship will excuse hints that he or one of his fellows have been negligent. And he prickled up again when Wexford said:

"How could he *know* it was a stroke without a postmortem?"

"God give me patience! He saw her before she was dead, didn't he? He got there about half an hour before she died. There are unmistakable signs of stroke, Reg. An experienced medical man couldn't fail to recognise them. The patient is unconscious, the face flushed, the pulse slow, the breathing stertorous with a puffing of the cheeks during expiration. The only possible confusion is with alcoholic poisoning, but in alcoholic poisoning the pupils of the eyes are widely dilated whereas in apoplexy or stroke they're contracted. Does that satisfy you?"

"Well, OK, it was a stroke, but aren't I right in thinking a stroke can be the consequence of something else, of an operation, for instance, or in the case of a young woman, of childbirth, or in an old person even of bedsores?"

"Old Ivy Wrangton didn't have bedsores and she hadn't had a baby for seventy years. She had a stroke because she was ninety-two and her arteries were worn out. 'The days of our age'," quoted the doctor solemnly, " 'are threescore years and ten, and though men be so strong that they come to fourscore years, yet is their strength then by labour and sorrow.' She'd reached fourscore years and twelve and she was worn out." He had been pacing up and down, getting heated, but now came to sit on the edge of his desk, a favourite perch of his. "A damn good thing she was cremated," he said. "That puts out of court all the ghastliness of exhumation and cutting her up. She was a remarkable old woman, you know, Reg. Tough as old boots. She told me once about having her first baby. She was eighteen, out scrubbing the doorstep when she had a labour pain. Indoors she went, called her mother to fetch the midwife and lay down on her bed. The baby was born after two more pains, and the daughter came even easier."

"Yes, I heard there'd been another child." Wexford saw the absurdity of referring to someone who must necessarily be in his seventies as a child. "Mrs. Betts has a brother?" he corrected himself.

"*Had*. He died last winter. He was an old man, Reg, and he'd been bronchial all his life. Seventy-four *is* old till you start comparing it with Mrs. Wrangton's age. She was so proud of her good health, boasted about never being ill. I used to drop in every three months or so as a matter of routine, and when I'd ask her how she was she'd say, I'm fine, doctor, I'm in the pink.'"

"But I understand she'd had some illness connected with an allergy?" Wexford was clutching at straws. "Nurse Radcliffe told me about it. I've been wondering if anything to do with that could have contributed to . . . ?"

"Of course not," the doctor cut in. "How could it? That was when she was middle-aged and the so-called illness was an asthmatic attack with some swelling of the eyes and a bit of gastric trouble. I fancy she used to exaggerate it the way healthy people do when they're talking about the one little bit of illness they've ever had . . . Oh, here's Jim. I thought I'd heard his last patient leave."

Dr. Moss, small, dark and trim, came in from the corridor between the consulting rooms. He gave Wexford the very wide smile that showed thirty-two large white teeth which the chief inspector had never been able to precisely define as false, as crowns or simply as his own. The teeth were rather too big for Dr. Moss's face which was small and smooth and lightly tanned. His small black eyes didn't smile at all.

"Enter the villainous medico," he said, "who is notoriously in cahoots with greedy legatees and paranoid Post Office clerks. What evidence can I show you? The number of my Swiss bank account? Or shall I produce the hammer, a crafty tap. from which ensured an immediate subarachnoid haemorrhage?"

It is very difficult to counter this kind of facetiousness. Wexford knew he would only get more fatuous pleasantries, heavy irony, outrageous confessions, if he attempted to rebut any of it or if he were to assure Moss that this wasn't what he had meant at all. He smiled stiffly, tapping his feet against the leg of Crocker's desk, while Dr. Moss elaborated on his fantasy of himself as corrupt, a kind of latter-day William Palmer, poison-bottle-happy and ever-ready with his hypodermic to gratify the impatient next-of-kin. At length, unable to bear any more of it, Wexford cut across the seemingly interminable harangue and said to Crocker:

"You witnessed her will, I understand?"

"I and that busybody Radcliffe, that's right. If you want to know what's in it, the house and three thousand pounds go to Doreen Betts, and the residue to another patient of mine, a Mrs. Parrish. Residue would have been about fifteen hundred at that time, Mrs. Wrangton told me, but considering her money was in a building society and she managed to save out of her pension and her annuity, I imagine it'll be a good deal more by now."

Wexford nodded. By now Dr. Moss had dried up, having run out, presumably, of subject matter and witticisms. His teeth irradiated his face like lamps, and when his mouth was closed he looked rather ill-tempered and sinister. Wexford decided to try the direct and simple approach. He apologised.

"I'd no intention of suggesting you'd been negligent, Dr. Moss. But put yourself in my position . . ."

"Impossible!"

"Very well. Let me put it this way. Try to understand that in my position I had no choice but to make enquiries."

"Mrs. Betts might try an action for slander. She can count on my support. The Bettses had neither the opportunity nor the motive to do violence to Mrs. Wrangton, but a bunch of tongue-clacking old witches are allowed to take their characters away just the same."

"Motive," said Wexford gently, "I'm afraid they did have, the straightforward one of getting rid of Mrs. Wrangton who had become an encumbrance to them, and of inheriting her house."

"Nonsense." Momentarily the teeth showed in a white blaze. "They were going to get rid of her in any case. They would have had the house to themselves in any case. Mrs. Wrangton was going into a nursing home." He paused, enjoying the effect of what he had said. "For the rest of her days," he added with a touch of drama.

Crocker shifted off the edge of the desk. "I never knew that."

"No? Well, it was you who told her about a new nursing home opening in Stowerton, or so she said. She told me all about it that day Mrs. Betts called me when you'd gone away. Sometime at the end of May it was. She was having the house decorated for her daughter and son-in-law prior to her leaving."

"Did she tell you that too?" asked Wexford.

"No, but it was obvious. I can tell you exactly what happened during that visit if it makes you happy. That interfering harpy, Radcliffe, had just been bathing her, and when she'd dressed her she left. Thank God. I'd never met Mrs. Wrangton before. There was nothing wrong with her, bar extreme old age and her blood pressure up a bit, and I was rather narked that Mrs. Betts had called me out. Mrs. Wrangton said her daughter got nervous when she slept late in the mornings as she'd done that day and the day before. Wasn't to be wondered at, she said, considering she'd been sitting up in bed watching the World Cup on television till all hours. Only Mrs. Betts and her husband didn't know that and I wasn't to tell them. Well, we had a conspiratorial laugh over that, I liked her, she was a game old dear, and then she started talking about the nursing home—what's it called? Springfield? Sunnyside?"

"Summerland," said Dr. Crocker.

"Cost you a lot, that will, I said, and she said she'd got a good bit coming in which would die with her anyway. I assumed she meant an annuity. We talked for about five minutes and I got the impression she'd been tossing around this nursing home idea for months. I asked her what her daughter thought and she said . . ."

"Yes?" prompted Wexford.

"Oh, my God, people like you make one see sinister nuances in the most innocent remarks. It's just that she said, You'd reckon Doreen'd be only too glad to see the back of me, wouldn't you? I mean, it rather implied she wouldn't be glad. I don't know what she was inferring and I didn't ask. But you can rest assured Mrs. Betts had no motive for killing her mother. Leaving sentiment apart, it was all the same to her whether her mother was alive or dead. The Bettses would still have got the house and after her death Mrs. Wrangton's capital. The next time I saw her she was unconscious, she was dying. She did die, at seven-thirty, on June 2nd."

Both Wexford's parents had died before he was forty. His wife's mother had been dead twenty years, her father fifteen. None of these people had been beyond their seventies, so therefore Wexford had no personal experience of the geriatric problem. It seemed to him that for a woman like Mrs. Wrangton, to end one's days in a nursing home with companionship and good nursing and in pleasant surroundings was not so bad a fate. And an obvious blessing to the daughter and son-in-law whose affection for a parent might be renewed when they only encountered her for an hour or so a week. No, Doreen Betts and her husband had no motive for helping Mrs. Wrangton out of this world, for by retiring to Summerland she wouldn't even make inroads into that three or four thousand pounds of capital. Her pension and her annuity would cover the fees. Wexford wondered what those fees would be, and remembered vaguely from a few years back hearing a figure of twenty pounds a week mentioned in a similar connection. Somebody's old aunt, some friend of his wife's. You'd have to allow for inflation, of course, but surely it would cost no more than thirty pounds a week now. With the Retirement Pension at eighteen pounds and the annuity worth, say, another twenty, Mrs. Wrangton could amply have afforded Summerland.

But she had died first—of natural causes. It no longer mattered that she and Harry Betts hadn't been on speaking terms, that no one had fetched Elsie Parrish, that Dr. Moss had been called out to visit a healthy woman, that Mrs. Betts had given orders to stop the painting. There was no motive. Eventually the tongues would cease to wag, Mrs. Wrangton's will would be proved, and the Bettses settle down to enjoy the rest of their lives in their newly decorated home.

Wexford put it out of his head, apart from wondering whether he should visit Castle Road and drop a word of warning to the gossips. Immediately he saw how impossible this would be. The slander would be denied, and besides he hardly saw his function as extending so far. No, let it die a natural death—as Mrs. Wrangton had.

On Monday morning he was having breakfast, his wife reading a letter just come from her sister in Wales.

"Frances says Bill's mother has got to go into a nursing

home at last." Bill was Wexford's brother-in-law. "It's either that or Fran having her, which really isn't on."

Wexford, from behind his newspaper, made noises indicative of sympathy with and support for Frances. He was reading a verbatim report of the trial of some bank robbers.

"Ninety pounds a week," said Dora.

"What did you say?"

"I was talking to myself, dear. You read your paper."

"Did you say ninety pounds a week?"

"That's right. For the nursing home. I shouldn't think Bill and Fran could stand that for long. It's getting on for five thousand a year."

"But . . ." Wexford almost stammered, ". . . I thought a couple of years ago you said it was twenty a week for what's-her-name, Rosemary's aunt, wherever they put her?"

"Darling," said Dora gently, "first of all, that wasn't a couple of years ago, it was at least *twelve* years ago. And secondly, haven't you heard of the rising cost of living?"

An hour later he was in the matron's office at Summerland, having made no attempt to disguise who he was, but presenting himself as there to enquire about a prospective home for an aged relative of his wife's. Aunt Lilian. Such a woman had actually existed, perhaps still did exist in the remote Westmorland village from which the Wexfords had last heard of her in a letter dated 1959.

The matron was an Irishwoman, Mrs. Corrigan. She seemed about the same age as Nurse Radcliffe. At her knee stood a boy of perhaps six, at her feet, playing with a toy tractor, was another of three. Outside the window three little girls were trying to coax a black cat from its refuge under a car. You might have thought this was a children's home but for the presence of half a dozen old women sitting on the lawn in a half circle, dozing, muttering to themselves or just staring. The grounds were full of flowers, mauve and white lilac everywhere, roses coming out. From behind a hedge came the sound of a lawn mower, plied perhaps by the philoprogenitive Mr. Corrigan.

"Our fees are ninety-*five* pounds a week, Mr. Wexford," said the matron. "And with the extra for laundry and dry-cleaning, sure and you might say five thousand a year for a good round figure."

"I see."

"The ladies only have to share a room with one other lady. We bath them once a week and change their clothes once a week. And if you could please see to it your aunt only has synthetic fabrics, if you know what I mean, for the lot's popped in the washing machine all together. We like the fees a month in advance and paid on a banker's order, if you please."

"I'm afraid I don't please," said Wexford. "Your charges are more than I expected. I shall have to make other arrangements."

"Then there's no more to be said," said Mrs. Corrigan with a smile nearly equalling the candlepower of Dr. Moss's.

"Just out of curiosity, Mrs. Corrigan, how do your—er, guests meet your fees? Five thousand a year is more than most incomes would be equal to."

"Sure and aren't they widows, Mr. Wexford, and didn't their husbands leave them their houses? Mostly the ladies sell their houses, and with prices the way they are today that's enough to keep them in Summerland for four years or five."

Mrs. Wrangton had intended to sell her house, and she was having it re-decorated inside and out in order to get a better price. She had intended to sell the roof over the Bettses' heads—no wonder she had implied to Dr. Moss that Doreen Betts would be sorry to see the back of her. What a woman! What malevolence at ninety-two! And who could have said she wouldn't have been within her moral as well as her legal rights to sell? It was her house. Doreen Wrangton might long ago have found a home of her own, ought perhaps to have done so, and as Doreen Betts might have expected her husband to provide one for her. It is universally admitted to be wrong to anticipate stepping into dead men's shoes. And yet what a monstrous revenge to have on an uncongenial son-in-law, a not always co-operative daughter. There was a subtlety about it that evoked Wexford's admiration nearly as much as its cruelty aroused his disgust. It was a motive all right, and a strong one.

So at last he had found himself in Castle Road, in the Bettses' living room, confronting an elderly orphan and her husband. The room was papered in a silvery oyster colour, the woodwork ivory. He was sure that that door had never previously sported a shade lighter than chocolate brown, just as the hall walls had, until their recent coat of magnolia, been gloomily clothed in dark Lincrusta.

When the two of them had protested bitterly about the gossip and the apparent inability of the police to get their priorities right, Doreen Betts agreed without too much mutiny to answer Wexford's questions. To the first one she reacted passionately.

"Mother would never have done it. I know she wouldn't, it was all bluff with her. Even Mother wouldn't have been that cruel."

Her husband pulled his moustache, slowly shuffling his slippered feet back and forth. His angry excitement had resulted in a drop of water appearing on the end of his nose. It hung there, trembling.

Doreen Betts said, "I knew she didn't mean to go ahead with it when I said, Can I tell the builders to leave the upstairs? And she said, I daresay. That's what she said, I daresay, she said, I'm not bothered either way. Of course she wouldn't have gone ahead with it. You don't even get a room to yourself in that place. Ninety-five pounds a week! They'll put you to bed at eight o'clock, Mother, I said, so don't think they'll let you sit up till all hours watching TV."

"Quite right," said Harry Betts ambiguously.

"Why, if we'd known Mother meant to do a thing like that, we could have lived in Harry's flat when we got married. He had a nice little flat over the freezer centre in the High Street. It wasn't just one room like Mother went about saying, it was a proper flat, wasn't it, Harry? What'd we have done if Mother'd done a thing like that? We'd have had nowhere." Her husband's head-shaking, the trembling droplet, the fidgety feet, seemed suddenly to unnerve her. She said to him, distress in her voice, "I'm going to have a little talk to the officer on my own, dear."

Wexford followed her into the room where Mrs. Wrangton had slept for the last years of her life. It was on the ground floor at the back, presumably originally designated as a dining room, with a pair of windows looking out onto a long narrow concrete terrace and a very long, very narrow garden. No re-decorations had been carried out here. The walls were papered in a pattern of faded nasturtiums, the woodwork grained to look like walnut. Mrs. Wrangton's double bed was still there, the mattress uncovered, a pile of folded blankets on top of it. There was a television set in this room as well as in the front room, and it had been placed so that the occupant of the bed could watch it.

"Mother came to sleep down here a few years back," said Mrs. Betts. "There's a toilet just down the passage. She couldn't manage the stairs any more except when nurse helped her." She sat on the edge of the mattress, nervously fingering a cage-like object of metal bars. "I'll have to see about her walking frame going back, I'll have to get on to the welfare people." Her hands resting on it, she said dolefully, "Mother hated Harry. She always said he wasn't good enough for me. She did everything she could to stop me marrying him." Mrs. Betts's voice took on a rebellious girlish note. "I think it's awful having to ask your mother's consent to marry when you're sixty-five, don't you?"

At any rate, he thought, she had gone ahead without receiving it. He looked wonderingly at this grey wisp of a woman, seventy years old, who talked as if she were a fairy princess.

"You see, she talked for years of changing her will and leaving the house to my brother. It was after he died that the nursing home business started. She quarrelled outright with Harry. Elsie Parrish was in here and Mother accused Harry in front of her of only marrying me to get this place. Harry never spoke a word to Mother again, and quite right too. I said to Mother, You're a wicked woman, you promised me years ago I'd have this house and now you're going back on your word. Cheats never prosper, I said."

The daughter had inherited the mother's tongue. Wexford could imagine the altercations, overheard by visitors, by neighbours, which had contributed to the gossip. He turned to look at the framed photograph on a mahogany tallboy. A wedding picture, *circa* 1903. The bride was seated, lilies in her lap under a bolster of a bosom hung with lace and pearls. The bridegroom stood behind her, frock coat, black handlebar moustache. Ivy Wrangton must have been seventeen, Wexford calculated, her face plain, puffy, young, her figure modishly pouter-pigeon-like, her hair in that most unflattering of fashions, the cottage loaf. She had been rather plump then, but thin, according to Nurse Radcliffe in old age. Wexford said quietly, apparently idly:

"Mrs. Betts, why did you send for Dr. Moss on May 23rd? Your mother wasn't ill. She hadn't complained of feeling ill."

She held the walking frame, pushing it backwards and forwards. "Why shouldn't I? Dr. Crocker was away. Elsie came in at nine and Mother was still asleep, and Elsie said it wasn't right the amount she slept. We couldn't wake her, though we shook her, we were so worried. I wasn't to know she'd get up as fit as a flea ten minutes after I'd phoned for him, was I?"

"Tell me about the day your mother died, Mrs. Betts, Friday, June 2nd," he said, and it occurred to him that no one had yet told him anything much about that day.

"Well . . ." Her mouth trembled and she said quickly, "You don't think Harry did anything to Mother, do you? He wouldn't, I swear he wouldn't."

"Tell me about that Friday."

She made an effort to control herself, clenching her hands on the metal bar. "We wanted to go to a whist drive. Elsie came round in the morning and I said, if we went out would she sit with Mother, and she said, OK, of course she would if I'd just give her a knock before we left." Mrs. Betts sighed and her voice steadied. "Elsie lives two doors down. She and Mother'd been pals for years and she always came to sit with her when we went out. Though it's a lie," her old eyes flashing like young ones, "to say we were always out. Once in a blue moon we went out."

Wexford's eyes went from the pudding-faced girl in the photograph, her mouth smug and proud even then, to the long strip of turfed-over garden—why did he feel Betts had done that turfing, had uprooted flowers?—and back to the nervous little woman on the mattress edge.

"I gave Mother her lunch and she was sitting in the front room, doing a bit of knitting. I popped down to Elsie's and rang her bell but she can't have heard it, she didn't come. I rang and rang and I thought, well, she's gone out, she's forgotten and that's that. But Harry said, Why not go out just the same? The painter was there, he was only a bit of a boy, twenty, twenty-two, but he and Mother got on a treat, a sight better than her and I ever did, I can tell you. So the upshot was, we went off and left her there with the painter—what was he called? Ray? Rafe? No, Roy, that was it, Roy—with Roy doing the hall walls. She was OK, fit as a flea. It was a nice day so I left all the windows open because that paint did smell. I'll never forget the way she spoke to me before I left. That was the last thing she ever said to me. Doreen, she said, you ought to be lucky at cards. You haven't been very lucky in love. And she laughed and I'll swear Roy was laughing too."

You're building an edifice of motives for yourself, Mrs. Betts, reflected Wexford. "Go on," was all he said.

She moved directly into hearsay evidence, but Wexford didn't stop her. "That Roy closed the door to keep the smell out, but he popped in a few times to see if Mother was all right. They had a bit of a chat, he said, and he offered to make her a cup of tea but she didn't want any.

Then about half-past three Mother said she'd got a headache—that was the onset of the stroke but she didn't
know that, she put it down to the paint—and would he
fetch her a couple of her paracetamols from the bathroom.
So he did and he got her a glass of water and she said
she'd try and have a sleep in her chair. Anyway, the next
thing he knew she was out in the hall walking with her
walking frame, going to have a lay-down on her bed, she
said.

"Well, Harry and me came in at five-thirty and Roy
was just packing up. He said Mother was asleep on her
bed, and I just put my head round the door to check.
She'd drawn the curtains." Mrs. Betts paused, burst out,
"To tell you the honest truth, I didn't look too closely. I
thought, well, thank God for half an hour's peace to have
a cup of tea in before she starts picking on Harry. It was
just about a quarter to seven, ten to seven, before I went
in again. I could tell there was something going on, the
way she was breathing, sort of puffing out her cheeks, and
red in the face. There was blood on her lips." She looked
fearfully at Wexford, looked him in the eye for the first
time. "I wiped that clean before I called the doctor, I
didn't want him seeing that.

"He came straightaway. I thought maybe he'd call an
ambulance but he didn't. He said she'd had a stroke and
when people had strokes they shouldn't be moved. We
stayed with her—well, doctor and I stayed with her—but
she passed away just before half-past."

Wexford nodded. Something about what she had said
was wrong. He felt it. It wasn't that she had told a lie,
though she might well have done, but something else,
something that rang incongruously in that otherwise com-
monplace narrative, some esoteric term in place of a
household word. . . . He was checking back, almost

there, when a footstep sounded in the hall, the door opened and a face appeared round it.

"There you are, Doreen!" said the face which was very pretty considering its age. "I was just on my way to—Oh, I beg your pardon, I'm intruding."

"That's all right," said Mrs. Betts. "You can come in, Elsie." She looked blankly at Wexford, her eyes once more old and tired. "This is Mrs. Parrish."

———————◆———————

Elsie Parrish, Wexford decided, looked exactly as an old lady should. She had a powdery, violet cashew, creamy smell, which might equally well have been associated with a very clean baby. Her legs were neat and shapely in grey stockings, her hands in white gloves with tiny darns at the fingertips, her coat silky navy-blue over blue flowery pleats, and her face withered rose leaves with rouge on. The bouffant mass of silvery hair was so profuse that from a distance it might have been taken for a white silk turban. She and Wexford walked down the street together towards the shops, Elsie Parrish swinging a pink nylon string bag.

"It's wicked the way they gossip. You can't understand how people can be so evil-minded. You'll notice how none of them are able to say how Doreen gave Ivy a stroke when she wasn't even there." Mrs. Parrish gave a dry satirical laugh. "Perhaps they think she bribed that poor young man, the painter, to give Ivy a fright. I remember my mother saying that fright could give you a stroke—an apoplexy, she called it—or too much excitement or drinking too much or over-eating even."

To his surprise, because this isn't what old ladies of elegant appearance usually do or perhaps should do, she opened her handbag, took out a packet of cigarettes and put one between her lips. He shook his head when the packet was offered to him, watched her light the cigarette with a match from a matchbook with a black shiny cover. She puffed delicately. He didn't think he had ever before seen someone smoke a cigarette while wearing white gloves. He said:

"Why didn't you go round and sit with Mrs. Wrangton, that afternoon, Mrs. Parrish?"

"The day she died, you mean?"

"Yes." Wexford had the impression she didn't want to answer, she didn't want to infer anything against Doreen Betts. She spoke with care.

"It's quite true I'm getting rather deaf." He hadn't noticed it. She had heard everything he said, in the open noisy street, and he hadn't raised his voice. "I don't always hear the bell. Doreen must have rung and I didn't hear. That's the only explanation."

Was it?

"I thought she and Harry had changed their minds about going out." Elsie Parrish put the cigarette to her lips between thumb and forefinger. "I'd give a lot," she said, "to be able to go back in time. I wouldn't hesitate this time, I'd go round and check on Ivy whether Doreen had asked me or not."

"Probably your presence would have made no difference," he said, and then, "Mrs. Betts had told the builders not to do any work upstairs . . ."

She interrupted him. "Maybe it didn't need it. I've never been upstairs in Ivy's house, so I couldn't say. Besides, when she'd sold it the new people might have had their own ideas, mightn't they? They might have wanted to do their own decorating."

They were standing still now on the street corner, he about to go in one direction, she in the other. She dropped the cigarette end, stamped it out over-thoroughly with a high heel. From her handbag she took a small lacy handkerchief and dabbed her nostrils with it. The impression was that the tears, though near, would be restrained. "She left me two thousand pounds. Dear Ivy, she was so kind and generous. I knew I was to have something, I didn't dream as much as that." Elsie Parrish smiled, a watery, girlish, rueful smile, but still he was totally unprepared for what she said next. "I'm going to buy a car."

His eyebrows went up.

"I've kept my licence going. I haven't driven since my husband died and that's twenty-two years ago. I had to sell our car and I've always longed and longed for another." She really looked as if she had, a yearning expression crumpling the roses still further. "I'm going to have my own dear little car!" She was on the verge of executing a dance on the pavement. "And dear Ivy made that possible!" Anxiously: "You don't think I'm too old to drive?"

Wexford did, but he only said that this kind of judgement wasn't really within his province. She nodded, smiled again, whisked off surprisingly fast into the corner supermarket. Wexford moved more slowly and thoughtfully away, his eyes down. It was because he was looking down that he saw the matchbook, and then he remembered fancying he had seen her drop something when she got out that handkerchief.

She wasn't in the shop. She must have left by the other exit into the High Street and now she was nowhere to be seen. Deciding that matchbooks were in the category of objects which no one much minds losing, Wexford dropped it into his pocket and forgot it.

"You want Roy?"

"That's right," said Wexford.

The foreman, storekeeper, proprietor, whatever he was, didn't ask why. "You'll find him," he said, "doing the Snowcem on them flats up the Sewingbury Road."

Wexford drove up there. Roy was a gigantic youth, broad-shouldered, heavily muscled, with an aureole of thick curly fair hair. He came down the ladder and said he'd just been about to knock off for his tea break, anyway. There was a carmen's café conveniently near. Roy lit a cigarette, put his elbows on the table.

"I never knew a thing about it till I turned up there the next day."

"But surely when Mrs. Betts came in the afternoon before she asked you how her mother had been?"

"Sure she did. And I said the truth, that the old lady'd got a headache and asked for something for it and I'd given it her, and then she'd felt tired and gone in for a lay-down. But there was no sign she was *dying*. My God, that'd never have crossed my mind."

A headache, Wexford reflected, was often one of the premonitory signs of a cerebral haemorrhage. Roy seemed to read his thoughts, for he said quickly:

"She'd had a good many headaches while I was in the place working. Them non-drip plastic-based paints have got a bit of a smell to them, used to turn *me* up at first. I mean, you don't want to get thinking there was anything out of the way in her having an aspirin and laying down, guv. That'd happened two or three times while I was there. And she'd shovel them aspirins down, swallow four as soon as look at you."

Wexford said, "Tell me about that afternoon. Did anyone come into the house between the time Mr. and Mrs. Betts went out and the time they got back?"

Roy shook his head. "Definitely not, and I'd have known. I was working on the hall, see? The front door was wide open on account of the smell. Nobody could have come in there without my seeing, could they? The other old girl—Mrs. Betts, that is—she locked the back door before she went out and I hadn't no call to unlock it. What else d'you want to know, guv?"

"Exactly what happened, what you and Mrs. Wrangton talked about, the lot."

Roy swigged his tea, lit a fresh cigarette from the stub of the last. "I got on OK with her, you know. I reckon she reminded me of my gran. It's a funny thing, but everyone got on OK with her bar her own daughter and the old man. Funny old git, isn't he? Gave me the creeps. Well, to what you're asking, I don't know that we talked much. I was painting, you see, and the door to the front room was shut. I looked in a couple of times. She was sitting there knitting, watching cricket on the TV. I do remember she said I was making a nice job of the house and it was a pity she wouldn't be there to enjoy it. Well, I thought she meant she'd be dead, you know the way they talk, and I said, Now come on, Mrs. Wrangton, you mustn't talk like that. That made her laugh. She said, I don't mean that, you naughty boy, I mean I'm going into a nursing home and I've got to sell the place, didn't you know? No, I said, I didn't, but I reckoned it'd fetch a packet, big old house like that, twenty thousand at least, I said, and she said she hoped so."

Wexford nodded. So Mrs. Wrangton had intended to go ahead with her plans, and Doreen Betts's denial had either been purposeful lying to demolish her motive or a post-mortem white-washing of her mother's character. For it had certainly been black-hearted enough, he thought, quite an act it had been, that of deliberately turning your own daughter and her husband out of their home. He looked back to Roy.

"You offered to make her tea?"

"Yeah, well, the daughter, Mrs. Betts, said to make myself and her a cup of tea if she wanted, but she didn't want. She asked me to turn off the TV and then she said she'd got a headache and would I go to the bathroom cupboard and get her aspirins? Well, I'd seen Mrs. Betts do it often enough, though I'd never actually . . ."

"You're sure she said aspirins?" Quite suddenly Wexford knew what it was that had seemed incongruous to him in Mrs. Betts's description of her mother's last afternoon of life. Doreen Betts had specified paracetamol instead of the common household remedy. "You're sure she used that word?" he said.

Roy pursed his mouth. "Well, now you mention it, I'm not sure. I reckon what she said was, my tablets or the tablets for my head, something like that. You just do say aspirins, don't you, like naturally? I mean, that's what everybody takes. Anyway, I brought them down, the bottle, and gave them to her with a glass of water, and she says she's going to have a bit of shut-eye in her chair. But the next thing I knew she was coming out, leaning on that walking frame the welfare people give her. I took four, Roy, she says, but my head's that bad, I reckon it's worse, and I'm ever so giddy. Well, I didn't think much of that, they're all giddy at that age, aren't they? I remember my gran. She says she's got ringing in her ears, so I said, I'll help you into your room, shall I? And I sort of give her my arm and helped her in and she lay down on the bed with all her things on and shut her eyes. The light was glaring so I pulled the curtains over and then I went back to my painting. I never heard another thing till Mrs. Betts and the old boy come in at half five . . ."

Wexford closed *Practical Forensic Medicine* by Francis
E. Camps and J. M. Cameron and made his way back to
Castle Road. He had decided to discuss the matter no further with Mrs. Betts. The presence of her husband,
shuffling about almost silently in his furry slippers, his
feet like the paws of an old hibernating animal, rather un-
nerved him. She made no demur at his proposal to remove from the bathroom cabinet the prescription bottle
of pain-killing tablets, labelled: Mrs. I. Wrangton, Paracetamols.

Evening surgery had only just begun. Wexford went
home for his dinner, having sent two items away for
fingerprint analysis. By eight-thirty he was back in the
surgery building and again Dr. Crocker had finished first.
He groaned when he saw Wexford.

"What is it now, Reg?"

"Why did you prescribe paracetamol for Mrs. Wrangton?"

"Because I thought it suitable for her, of course. She
was allergic to aspirin."

Wexford looked despairingly at his friend. "Now he
tells me. I'd rather gathered it. I mean, today I caught on,
but you might have told me."

"For God's sake! You *knew*. You said to me, Nurse
Radcliffe told me all about it. Those were your words.
You said . . ."

"I thought it was asthma."

Crocker sat on the edge of his desk. "Look, Reg, we've
both been barking up the wrong trees. There was asthma
in Mrs. Wrangton's family. Mrs. Betts has nettle rash, her
brother was a chronic asthmatic. People with asthma or a
family history of asthma are sometimes allergic to acetylsalicylic acid or aspirin. In fact, about ten per cent of
such people are thought to have the allergy. One of the

reactions of the hypersensitive person to aspirin is an asthmatic attack. That's what Mrs. Wrangton had when she was in her forties, that and haematemesis. Which means," he added kindly for the layman, "bringing up blood from an internal haemorrhage."

"OK, I'm not bone ignorant," Wexford snapped, "and I've been reading up hypersensitivity to acetylsalicylic acid . . ."

"Mrs. Wrangton couldn't have had aspirin poisoning," said the doctor quickly. "There were never any aspirins in the house. Mrs. Betts was strict about that."

They were interrupted by the arrival of smiling Dr. Moss. Wexford wheeled round on him.

"What would you expect to be the result of—let me see —one point two grammes of acetylsalicylic acid on a woman of ninety-two who was hypersensitive to the drug?"

Moss looked at him warily. "I take it this is academic?" Wexford didn't answer. "Well, it'd depend on the degree of hypersensitivity. Nausea, maybe, diarrhoea, dizziness, tinnitus—that's ringing in the ears—breathing difficulties, gastric haemorrhages, oedema of gastric mucosa, possible rupture of the oesophagus. In a person of that age, consequent upon such a shock and localised haemorrhages, I suppose a brain haemorrhage. . . ." He stopped, realising what he had said.

"Thanks very much," said Wexford. "I think you've more or less described what happened to Mrs. Wrangton on June 2nd after she'd taken four three hundred milligram tablets of aspirin."

———◆———

Dr. Moss was looking stunned. He looked as if he would never smile again. Wexford passed an envelope to Crocker.

"Those are aspirins?"

Crocker looked at them, touched one to his tongue. "I suppose so, but . . ."

"I've sent the rest away to be analysed. To be certain. There were fifty-six in the bottle."

"Reg, it's unthinkable there could have been a mistake on the part of the pharmacist, but just supposing by a one in a million chance there was, she couldn't have taken forty-four tablets of aspirin. Not even over the months she couldn't."

"You're being a bit slow," said Wexford. "You prescribed one hundred paracetamol, and one hundred paracetamol were put into that bottle at Fraser's, the chemist's. Between the time the prescription was made up and the day before, or a few days before, or a week before, she died, she took forty tablets of paracetamol, leaving sixty in the bottle. But on June 2nd she took four tablets of aspirin. Or, to put it bluntly, some time before June 2nd someone removed those sixty tablets of paracetamol and substituted sixty tablets of aspirin."

Dr. Moss found his voice. "That would be murder."

"Well . . ." Wexford spoke hesitantly. "The hypersensitivity might not have resulted in a stroke. The intent may only have been to cause illness of a more or less severe kind. Ulceration of the stomach, say. That would have meant hospitalisation for Mrs. Wrangton. On the Welfare State. No exorbitant nursing home fees to be paid there, no swallowing up of capital or selling of property. Later on, if she survived, she would probably have been transferred, again for free, to a geriatric ward in the same hospital. It's well-known that no private nursing home will take the chronically sick."

"You think Mrs. Betts . . . ?" Dr. Moss began.

"No, I don't. For two good reasons, Mrs. Betts is the

one person who wouldn't have done it this way. If she had wanted to kill her mother or to make her seriously ill, why go to all the trouble of changing over sixty tablets in a bottle, when she had only to give Mrs. Wrangton the aspirins in her hand? And if she had changed them, wouldn't she, immediately her mother was dead, have changed them back again?"

"Then who was it?"

"I shall know tomorrow," said Wexford.

Crocker came to him at his office in the police station.

"Sorry I'm late. I just lost a patient."

Wexford made sympathetic noises. Having walked round the room, eyed the two available chairs, the doctor settled for the edge of Wexford's desk.

"Yesterday," Wexford began, "I had a talk with Mrs. Elsie Parrish." He checked the doctor's exclamation and sudden start forward. "Wait a minute, Len. She dropped a matchbook before we parted. It was one of those with a glossy surface that very easily takes prints. I had the prints on it and those on the paracetamol bottle compared. There were Mrs. Betts's prints on the bottle, and a set that were presumably Mrs. Wrangton's, and a man's that were presumably the painter's. And there was also a very clear set identical to those on the matchbook.

"It was Elsie Parrish who changed those tablets, Len. She did it because she knew that Mrs. Wrangton fully intended to retire to Summerland and that the first money to go, perhaps before the house was sold, would be the few thousands of capital she and Doreen Betts were to share. Elsie Parrish had waited for years for that money, she wanted to buy a car. A few more years and if she herself survived it would be too late for driving cars. Besides, by then her legacy would have been swallowed up in nursing home fees."

"A nice old creature like that?" Crocker said. "That's no proof, her prints on the bottle. She'll have fetched that bottle often enough for old Ivy."

"No. She told me she had never been upstairs in Ivy Wrangton's house."

"Oh, God."

"I don't suppose she saw it as murder. It wouldn't seem like murder, or manslaughter, or grievous bodily harm, changing tablets over in a bottle." Wexford sat down, wrinkled up his face. He said crossly, dispiritedly, "I don't know what to do, Len. We've no way of proving Mrs. Wrangton died of aspirin poisoning. We can't exhume her, we can't analyse 'two handfuls of white dust shut in an urn of brass.' And even if we could, would we be so inhumane as to have a woman of—how old is Elsie Parrish?"

"Seventy-eight."

"Seventy-eight up in court on a murder charge. On the other hand, should she be allowed to profit from her crime? Should she be permitted to terrorise pedestrians in a smart little Ford Fiesta?"

"She won't," said Crocker.

Something in his voice brought Wexford to his feet. "Why? What d'you mean?"

The doctor slid lightly off the edge of the desk. "I told you I'd lost a patient. Elsie Parrish died last night. A neighbour found her and called me."

"Maybe that's for the best. What did she die of?"

"A stroke," said Crocker, and went.

Ginger and the Kingsmarkham Chalk Circle

"There's a girl downstairs, sir," said Polly Davies, "and she says someone's taken her baby out of its pram."

Chief Inspector Wexford had been contemplating a sheet of foolscap. On it, written by himself in the cause of crime prevention, was a politely worded request to the local authority, asking them to refrain from erecting scaffolding around their rented property a full nine months before building work was due to commence. Because of the scaffolding there had already been two burglaries and an assault on a young woman. He looked up from the paper, adjusted his thoughts and sighed.

"They will do it," he said. "Leave their babies about I mean. You'd never find them leaving their handbags outside shops."

"It was outside her flat, sir, not a shop, and the thing is, whoever took the baby left another one in its place."

———◆———

Slowly Wexford got up. He came round the desk and looked narrowly at Polly.

"Constable Davies, you have to be pulling my leg."

"No, sir, you know I wouldn't. She's a Mrs. Bond and she says that when she went downstairs to fetch in her pram, her baby had gone and another one been put there."

Wexford followed Polly down to the ground floor. In one of the interview rooms a girl was sitting at the bleak, rectangular, plastic-topped table, drinking tea and crying. She looked about nineteen. She had long straw-coloured hair and a small childish face, naive and innocent and frightened, and she was wearing blue denims and a tee-shirt with apples and oranges and cherries printed all over the front. From her appearance one would not have supposed her to be a mother. But also in the room was a baby. The baby, in short white frock and woolly coat and napkin and cotton socks, slept in the uneasy arms of Detective Constable Loring.

It had occurred to Wexford on the way down that women who have recently had babies are, or are said to be, prone to various kinds of mental disturbance, and his first thought was that Mrs. Bond might only think or only be saying that this child was not hers.

"Now, Mrs. Bond," he began, "this is a strange business. Do you feel like telling me about it?"

"I've told it all," she said.

"Well, yes, but not to me. Why not start by telling me where you live and where your baby was?"

She gulped. She pushed the teacup away. "Greenhill Court. We're on the fifth floor. We haven't got a balcony or anything. I have to go all the way down in the lift to put Karen out in her pram. She's got to have fresh air. And when she's there I can't watch her all the time. I can't even see her from my lounge on account of it looks out over the car park."

"So you put her out in the pram this afternoon," said Wexford. "What time would that have been?"

"It was just on two. I put the pram on the grass with

the cat net on it, and when I went to fetch it in at half-
past four the cat net was still on it and the baby was
asleep but it—it wasn't Karen!" She made little whimper-
ing noises that exploded in a sob. "It wasn't Karen, it was
that baby he's holding!"

The baby woke up and also began to cry. Loring wrinkled up his nose and shifted his left hand from under its
buttocks. His eyes appealed to Polly who nodded and left
the room.

"So what did you do?" said Wexford.

"I didn't even go back upstairs. I got hold of the pram
and I pushed it and I started to run and I ran all the way
down here to you."

He was touched by her childish faith. In real or imagi-
nary trouble, at time of fear, she ran to those whom her
sheltered small-town upbringing had taught her to trust,
the kindly helmeted man in blue, the strong arm of the
law. Not for her the grosser cynical image her city-bred
contemporaries held of brutal and bribable policemen.

"Mrs. Bond," he said, and then, "What's your first
name?"

"Philippa. I'm called Pippa."

"Then I'll call you that if you don't mind. Describe
your baby to me, will you, Pippa? Is she dark or fair?
How old is she?"

"She's two months old—well, nine weeks. She's got blue
eyes, she's wearing a white frock." The voice broke and
trembled again. "And she's got the most beautiful red-
gold hair you've ever seen!"

Inevitably, Wexford's eyes went to the child in Loring's
arms whom this description seemed perfectly to fit. He
said gently to Pippa Bond, "Now you're quite sure you
aren't imagining all this? No one will be angry if you are,
we shall understand. Perhaps you worried or felt a bit

guilty about leaving Karen out of your sight for so long, and then when you came down you got a feeling she looked rather different from usual and . . ."

A wail of indignation and misery cut across the rest of what he had to say. The girl began to cry with long tearing sobs. Polly Davies came back, carrying a small square hand towel from the women's lavatory. She took the baby from Loring, laid it on its back on the table and undid the big safety pin above its navel. Pippa Bond flinched away from the baby as if it were carrying a disease.

"I'm not imagining it," she shouted at Wexford. "I'm not! D'you think I wouldn't know my own baby? D'you think I wouldn't know my Karen from *that?*"

Polly had folded the towel cornerwise. She moved a little so that Wexford could see the baby's waving legs and bare crotch. "Whoever this baby is, sir, it isn't Karen. Look for yourself—it's a boy."

Trevor Bond was fetched from the Stowerton estate agent's where he worked. He looked very little older than his wife. Pippa clung to him, crying and inarticulate, and over her bent head he cast despairing eyes at the policemen.

He had arrived in a car driven by a young woman he said was his sister-in-law, Pippa's sister, who also lived at Greenhill Court with her husband. She sat stiffly at the wheel, giving Pippa no more than a nod and what seemed like a shrug of exasperation when she came out of the police station with Trevor's arm round her. Susan Rains, her name was, and a quarter of an hour later it was she who was showing Loring and Sergeant Martin just where the pram had stood on the lawn between the block of flats and the main road from Kingsmarkham to Stowerton.

While this thin red-haired girl castigated her sister's negligence and put forward her own theories as to where Karen might be, Dr. Moss arrived with sedation for Pippa, though she had become calmer once she understood no one would expect her to have charge of the changeling boy.

His fate was removal to a Kingsmarkham Borough nursery for infants in the care of the local authority.

"Poor lamb," said the children's officer Wexford spoke to. "I expect Kay will be able to take him in Bystall Lane. There's no one to fetch him, though, they've got ten to bath and get to bed down there."

Young Ginger, Wexford had begun to call him. He was a fine-looking baby with large eyes, strong pudgy features, and hair of a curious pale red, the colour of a new raw carrot. To Wexford's not inexperienced eye, he looked older than the missing Karen, nearer four months than two. His eyes were able to focus firmly, and now they focussed on the chief inspector, a scrutiny which moved the baby to yell miserably. Young Ginger buried his face in Polly's boyish bosom, crying and searching for sustenance.

"You don't know what they're thinking, do you, sir?" Polly said. "Just because we can't remember anything about when we were his age we sort of think babies don't feel much or notice things. But suppose what they feel is so awful they sort of block it off just so as they won't be able to remember? Suppose it's dreadful pain being separated from your mother and not being able to say and— Oh, I don't know, but does anyone think of these things, sir?"

"Well, psychiatrists do," said Wexford, "and philosophers, I expect, but not many ordinary people like us.

You'll have to remember it when you have babies of your own. Now take him down to Bystall Lane, will you?"

A few minutes after she had gone Inspector Burden came in. He had heard the story downstairs but had not entirely believed it. It was the part about putting another baby in Karen's place that he couldn't believe, he told Wexford. He hadn't either, said Wexford, but it was true.

"You can't think of a reason why anyone would do such a thing," said Burden. "You can't think of a single reason why even a mentally disturbed person would do such a thing."

"I suppose," said Wexford, "that by 'you' you mean yourself or 'one' because *I* can think of several reasons for doing it. First of all, you've got to take some degree of mental disturbance for granted here. Well-adjusted normal people don't steal other people's babies, let alone exchange them. It's going to be a woman. It's a woman who's done it because she wants to be rid of that particular child, yet she must have a child. Agreed?"

"Right," said Burden. "Why?"

"She has to show it to someone else," Wexford said slowly, as if thinking aloud, "someone who expects to see a baby nearer in age and appearance to Karen Bond than to young Ginger, or who expects a baby of Karen's sex. She may be a woman who has several sons and whose husband was away when the last one was born. She has told him he has a daughter, and to bear this out because she's afraid of him, she has to have a girl to produce for him. On the other hand, she may not be married. She may have told a boy friend or ex-boy friend the child is younger than it is in order to convince him of his paternity."

"I'm glad you mentioned mental disturbance," said Burden sarcastically.

"She may simply be exhausted by looking after a child who screams incessantly—young Ginger's got a good pair of lungs—so she exchanges him for a baby she believes won't scream. Or she may have been told that Ginger has some illness or even hereditary defect which frightened her so she wanted to be rid of him, but she still has to have a baby for her husband or mother or whoever to see."

Burden seemed to be considering this inventiveness with reluctant admiration but not much conviction. He said, "So what are we going to do about it?"

"I've taken everyone in the place off what they were doing and put them on to this. We're getting on to all the hospitals and GPs, the Registrar of births, and the post-natal and baby clinics. I think it has to be someone local, maybe even someone who knew the pram would be there because she'd seen it there before."

"And seen the baby who was in it before?" asked Burden, quirking up an eyebrow.

"Not necessarily. A pram with a cat net over and whose occupant can't be seen implies a very young baby." Wexford hesitated. "This is a hell of a lot more worrying," he said, "than a run-of-the-mill baby-snatching."

"Because Karen Bond's so young?" Burden hazarded.

"No, not that. Look, Mike, your typical baby-snatcher loves babies, she yearns for one of her own, and that's why she takes someone else's. But this one's *got* a baby of her own and one she dislikes enough to hand him over to a stranger. You can pretty well take it for granted the ordinary baby-snatcher will care for a child almost extravagantly well, but will this one? If she doesn't care for her own child, will she care for a substitute? I say it's worrying because we can be certain this woman's taken Karen for a purpose, a use, and what happens when that use is over?"

The block of flats in which the Bonds lived was not one of those concerning whose vulnerability to break-ins Wexford had been drafting his letter, but a privately owned five-storeyed building standing on what not long ago had been open green meadows. There were three such blocks, Greenhill, Fairlawn and Hillside Courts, interspersed with rows of weatherboarded town houses, and each block was separated from the main road to Stowerton only by a strip of lawn thirty feet deep. On this turf, a little way in from the narrow service road, Karen Bond's pram had stood.

Wexford and Burden talked to the porter who had charge of the three blocks. He had been cleaning a car in the car park at the relevant time and had noticed nothing. Wexford, going up in the Greenhill lift, commented to Burden that it was unfortunate children were forbidden to play on the lawns. They would have served as protection of Karen or at least as witnesses. There were a good many children on this new estate which was mainly occupied by young couples. Between two and four-thirty that afternoon the little ones had been cooped up in small rooms or out for walks with their mothers, the older ones at school.

Mrs. Louise Pelham had fetched her son and her next-door neighbour's two sons home from school, passing within a few feet of Karen's pram. That was at a quarter to four. She had glanced into the pram, as she always did, and now she said she remembered thinking Karen looked "funny." The baby in the pram had seemed to have a bigger face and redder hair than the one she had looked at when she passed on her way to the children's school half an hour before. Wexford felt that there was a real lead here, a pinpointing of the time of the substitution,

until he learned that Susan Rains had been with Mrs.
Pelham before him and told her the whole story in detail.

Susan Rains and her sister Pippa had each been married
at the age of eighteen, but Pippa at twenty already had a
baby while Susan, seven years older, was childless. She
was without a job too, it appeared, and at three years
short of thirty was leading the life of a middle-aged house-
proud gossip. She seemed very anxious to tell Wexford
and Burden that, in her opinion, her sister was far too
young to have a child, her brother-in-law too young to be
a father, and that they were both too irresponsible to look
after a baby. Pippa, she said, was always bringing Karen
round for her to mind, and now Wexford, who had been
wondering about the two folded napkins, the plastic spoon
and bottle of concentrated orange juice on Mrs. Rains's
spotless kitchen counter, understood why they were
there.

"Are you fond of babies, Mrs. Rains?" Wexford asked,
and got an almost frightening response.

Hard lines bit into Mrs. Rains's face and her redhead's
pale eyes flashed. "I'd be an unnatural woman if I wasn't,
wouldn't I?" What else she might have said—a defence?
An explanation?—was cut off by the arrival of a woman in
her late forties whom she introduced in a mutter as her
mother. It was left to Wexford to find out that this was
Mrs. Leighton who had left Pippa in a drugged sleep and
Trevor trying to answer Sergeant Martin's second spate of
questions.

Mrs. Leighton was sprightly and not too concerned.
"Well, babies that get taken out of prams, they always
turn up safe and sound, don't they?" Her hair was dyed to
a more glorious red than her daughter's natural shade.
She was on her way to babysit for her son and daughter-
in-law who had a six-month-old son, and she had just

looked in on Pippa to collect the one pound twenty she
owed her for dry-cleaning. Imagine what she'd felt, the
whole place full of policemen and Karen gone. She really
thought Trevor or Susan might have phoned her, and now
she was in two minds whether to go and babysit for Mark
or not. "But she's bound to turn up OK, isn't she?" she
said to Wexford.

Wexford said they must hope so, and then he and Burden left the two women to argue between themselves as
to which was the more important, keeping a promise to
the son or commiserating with the daughter.

The world, or this small corner of it, suddenly seemed
full of babies. From behind two doors on the ground floor
came the whimpers and low peevish grizzlings of infants
put unwillingly in their cots for the night. As they left by
the glass double doors, they passed on the step an ath-
letic-looking girl in sweater and denims with a very small
baby clamped to her chest in a canvas baby carrier. The
car park was filling as men returned home from work,
some of them commuters from London, and among them,
walking from a jaunty red sports car, a couple swinging
between them a baby in a shallow rush basket. Wexford
wondered just how many children under the age of two
lived in those flats and small neat houses. Nearly as many
as there were adults, he thought, and he stood aside to let
pass a girl pushing twins in a wide push-chair.

There was very little more that he could do that night
beyond embroiling himself in another discussion with
Burden as to the reason why. Burden put forward several
strange suggestions. Having previously declared that he
couldn't think of a single motive, he now posited that the
baby-snatcher was due to have her own baby immunised
against whooping cough on the following day. She had
read in the newspaper that this could cause brain damage

but was too diffident to refuse the immunisation, so planned to substitute someone else's baby for her own.

"The trouble with you unimaginative people," said Wexford, "is that when you do fantasise you really go crazy. She wants to protect her child from what's something like a one in a million chance of brain damage, but she doesn't mind entrusting him to the care of strangers who might do him far more harm."

"But the point is she knew they wouldn't do him harm. She'd know that what's happened is exactly what must happen, that he'd be brought to us and then put in the care of the local authority." Burden waited for some show of enthusiasm and when he didn't get it he went home. For three hours. At eleven that night he was destined to be called out again.

But not on account of Karen Bond.

In normal circumstances Sergeant Willoughby, going off duty, wouldn't have given a second glance at the Ford Transit parked under some overhanging bushes at the foot of Ploughman's Lane. But the sergeant's head, like those of most members of the Mid-Sussex Constabulary, was full of thoughts of missing children. He saw the van as a possible caravan substitute, and his mind went vaguely back to old tales of infants stolen by gypsies. He parked his scooter and went over to investigate.

The young man sitting in the driving seat switched on the ignition, put the van into gear and moved off as fast as he could on a roar of the engine. There was no real danger of his hitting Sergeant Willoughby, nor did that seem to have been his intention, but he passed within a yard or so of him and swung down the lane towards the town.

The nearest phone was in the sergeant's own home in Queen Street, and he went quickly to it.

But the Ford Transit turned out to have had nothing to do with Karen Bond. It was the getaway car for two men who were taking advantage of the absence of a Kingsmarkham stockbroker and his wife to remove a safe from their home.

Ploughman's Lane was Kingsmarkham's millionaire's row, and Stephen Pollard's house, pretentiously named Baron's Keep, by no means the smallest or most modest house in it. It was a nineteen-thirties palace of red brick and leaded lattices and neo-Tudor twisty chimneys. All the windows on the ground floor had stout bars to them, but there were no bars on the french window which led from the largest of the rear bedrooms on to a spacious balcony. When Burden and Loring got there they found signs that two men had climbed up to this balcony, ignored the thief-proof locks on the french window, and cut the glass neatly out of its frame with a glass cutter.

Where the safe had been in the study on the ground floor was now a gaping cavity. This room was said to be a precise replica of some writing room or den or hidey-hole of Mary Queen of Scots in Holyrood Palace, and the safe had been concealed behind a sliding door in the linenfold panelling. The thieves had chipped it out of its niche with a cold chisel and removed it bodily. Burden thought it must have been immensely heavy, which explained the need for having the van nearby.

Although the weather was dry, a long wet spell had only just ended. Deeply indented footprints, one set of a size eight shoe, the other of a size twelve, had ground into the flowerbed under the balcony. These same prints crossed the rear lawn to where there was a gate in the tall wattle fence, and alongside them went parallel grooves about two inches apart.

"I reckon," said Burden, "they had a set of those

wheels people have for pushing heavy luggage along. That's what they used. The sheer cheek of it!"

Loring shone his torch. "They rested it down here, sir, in front of the gate. Must have been a bit of a blow when they found their motor gone and they had to keep on wheeling."

In vain they searched the lane, the ditches and the copse which bordered the lane on one side. They didn't find the safe and no fingerprints were found on the window ledges or in the study at Baron's Keep. The thieves had worn gloves.

"And Big Feet," said Burden in the morning, "should have worn snow shoes. There aren't going to be many villains about with great plates of meat like that."

"I'd think of Lofty Peters first thing," said Wexford, "only he's inside."

"Well, he's not actually. He came out last week. But we were round at his place, knocking him up at midnight and waking all the neighbours, and there was no doubt where he'd been all evening. He was blind drunk, smashed out of his mind. I reckon this lot came down from London. Old Pollard's been shooting his mouth off around the City about his missus's diamonds and this is the outcome."

"The van was nicked," said Wexford. "I've just had a call from the super at Myringham. They found it ditched on the edge of a wood with the licence plates missing."

"What a lively time we are having," said Burden, and he looked out of the window at the geraniums on the forecourt and the shops opening, striped awnings gradually being unfurled, shoppers' cars moving in, the July sun spreading a great sheet of light and warmth across the Pomfret Road—and a little figure walking through it in unseasonable black. "My God," he said, "I don't believe it, not another one!"

Wexford got up and came over to the window. The small stout man in the black cassock was now on the forecourt, walking between the geranium tubs. In his arms was a bundle that was undoubtedly a baby. He was carrying the baby very confidently and securely as might be expected in one who so often performed the sacrament of baptism. Wexford watched him in silence, craning out to follow the priest's progress under the overhanging canopy and through the swing doors into the police station.

He said in a distant speculative voice, "You don't suppose, do you, Mike, that this is the latest craze? I mean, we've had wife-swapping, are we going to have baby-swapping? Maybe it's something that bored young housewives are going to take up instead of going to evening classes or playing with their deep freezes."

"Or maybe there's a maniac on the rampage who gets his kicks from changing them all round and confusing their mums."

"Musical babes," said Wexford. "Come on, let's go down and see." They descended to the foyer in the lift. "Good morning, Father. And who might this be?"

The priest in charge of the Catholic church of Our Lady of Loretto was leaning against the long parabola-shaped counter behind which the station sergeant, Sergeant Camb, presided. The sleeping baby in his arms was swathed, indeed tightly cocooned, in a clean pale blue cellular blanket. Only its face, fragile yet healthy-looking, and one hand were exposed. Thick dark lashes rested on the rose-leaf skin, but otherwise the child was fair, eyebrow-less and with fine downy hair as bright as a new copper coin. Holding it with tender firmness, Father Glanville looked round from his conversation with the sergeant to give Wexford a mystified grin, while Polly

Davies stroked the baby's tiny fingers with her own forefinger.

"Your guess is as good as mine, Mr. Wexford. I went over to the church just before nine and when I came back this little one was on the front steps of the presbytery. My lady help, Mrs. Bream, had come in by the back door and hadn't even noticed him."

"You found him just like that?" said Wexford. "Just wrapped in that blanket and lying on the doorstep."

"No indeed. He was wrapped in this blanket inside a cardboard box. The cardboard box," said Father Glanville, smiling, "is of the kind one sees in grocery supermarkets. This particular one has printed on it: Smith's Ready Salted Crisps, Ten Family Packs." He added rather anxiously, "I'm afraid I haven't brought it with me."

Wexford couldn't help laughing. "Well, don't throw it away. It's very likely a vital piece of evidence." He came closer to the child who slept on regardless of the talk and the four large alien presences. "You brought it straight here?"

"I brought *him* straight here," said Father Glanville with the faintest note of reproof in his voice. Wexford reflected that he ought to have known the priest would never refer to any human soul, however youthful, however unknown and unidentified, as "it," and then he said:

"I suppose he is a he? Blue blankets don't necessarily denote maleness, do they?"

The three men, for some obscure reason known to none of them, turned their eyes simultaneously on Polly Davies. And she, somehow recognising that to ascertain gender was her peculiar function, gently took the baby out of Father Glanville's arms, turned away and began unwrapping the blue blanket. The baby woke up and at once began a strenuous crying. Polly re-wrapped the blanket, set the child against her shoulder, her hand pressed against the four-inch wide back.

"This is a little girl, sir." She put the baby's cheek against her own. "Sir, don't you think it's Karen Bond? I'm sure it is, it must be." Her voice had a catch in it. To her own evident horror, there were tears coming into her eyes. "To think someone just dumped her, someone else's child, on a doorstep, in a cardboard box!"

"Well, the someone couldn't have left her in a better place, could she?" said Wexford with a grin at the priest. "Come now, Constable Davies, this is no way for a liberated woman to go on. Let us pull ourselves together and go and phone Mrs. Bond."

———————◆▶———————

Trevor and Pippa Bond arrived together, having again been brought to the police station in Susan Rains's car. The young husband was plainly terrified that the child would turn out not to be theirs, that their journey would prove to have been a cruel and vain awakening of hope, and for this reason he had tried to persuade his wife not to come. But she had come. Nothing could have kept her away, though she was fuddled and dazed still from Dr. Moss's sedatives.

But once she saw the baby the muzziness left her and the look went out of her eyes. She seized her in her arms, crushing her until Karen cried out and struggled with all her nine-week-old energy. Inscrutably, Susan Rains watched the little drama, watched her sister throw the blue blanket on to the floor, shuddering as she did so, watched the tears run down her cheeks on to the baby's head. Pippa began frenetically examining the white frock, the matinée jacket, the minute socks, as if hunting for visible germs.

"Why don't you burn the lot?" said Susan very coolly. "Then you won't have to worry."

Trevor Bond said quickly and awkwardly, "Well, thanks very much, thanks a lot. I'll just see these girls of mine home and then I'll get off to the office. We've got a lot on our plates, always have this time of the year."

"I'll take them back, Trev," said Susan. "You get off to work. And I'll phone Mother."

"I'd let Dr. Moss have a look at Karen if I were you," said Wexford. "She seems fine and I'm sure she is, but better be on the safe side."

They went on their way. Susan Rains walked a little behind the others, already marked for her role as the eternal aunt. Wexford's thoughts went to her nephew, her brother Mark's child, though he didn't know why he should think of him just then, and then to young Ginger, that grass orphan, down in Bystall Lane. He picked up the blanket—young Ginger's blanket?—and examined it, coming to the conclusion at the end of a few minutes' scrutiny of its texture and its label, that it was made of pure wool, had been manufactured in Wales, was old but clean and had been mended in one corner by someone who was no tyro when it came to handling a darning needle. From its honeycombing he picked a quantity of hairs. Most of these were baby hair, very fine red-gold filaments that might (or then again might not) all have come from the same child's scalp, but among them were a few coarser longer hairs that were clearly from a woman's head. A red-headed woman. He was thinking about the two red-headed women he had encountered during the time Karen was missing, when there came a knock at the door.

Wexford called, "Come in," and Sergeant Willoughby

first put his head round the door, then advanced a little sheepishly into the office. Behind him came Burden.

"The young chap I saw driving that van last night, sir," said Willoughby, "I knew his face was familiar, I knew I'd seen him before. Anyway, I've remembered who he is. Tony Jasper, sir. I'm certain of it."

"And am I supposed to know who Tony Jasper is?"

Burden said quickly, "You know his brother. His brother's Paddy Jasper."

"Paddy Jasper went up north."

"That's what they said," said Burden, "and maybe he did, but his girl friend's back living round here. You know Leilie Somers, he's lived with her on and off for years, ever since she left Stowerton Secondary Modern when she was sixteen."

"D'you know where she's living?"

"In one of those flats•over the shops in Roland Road," said Burden.

Roland Road was in Stowerton, running behind and parallel to the High Street. Wexford's driver took him and Burden along the High Street to reach it and, looking out of the window, Wexford saw Pippa Bond's mother walking along, shop-window-gazing and pushing a pram that was higher and grander than her daughter's and of a rich dark green colour. Its occupant was presumably her grandson. Mrs. Leighton was also dressed in dark green and her dyed hair looked redder than ever.

The car turned left, then right into Roland Road. The row of shops, eight of them, was surmounted by a squat upper floor of aimlessly peaked roofs and, on its façade, a useless adornment of green-painted studs and beams. The block had been put up at approximately the same period as Baron's Keep, the time which Wexford called the Great Tudor Revival. He remarked to Burden that the whole face of urban and semi-rural Britain would have been changed immeasurably for the better if architects in the third and fourth decades of the century had revived the Georgian instead of the Elizabethan. Think of it, he said, long elegant sash windows instead of poky casements, columns instead of half-timbering and pediments instead of gables. Burden didn't answer him. He had given a push to the door between the newsagent's and the pet food shop, and it gave under his hand and swung inwards.

The passage was rather dark. At the foot of the stairs was a pram from which a young woman was lifting a baby. She turned round as the light fell on her and said:

"Oh, hallo, I was just coming back to shut that. Were you wanting something?"

Burden was inspired. He said, remembering Leilie Somers's character, guessing at her hopes and fears, "We're looking for Mrs. Jasper."

The girl knew at once whom he meant. "Leilie's door's the one on the right at the top of the stairs." The baby on her hip, she parked the pram a little way down the passage, pulled and fastened the cover up over it.

"Do you know if her husband's at home?"

Her reply came guilelessly up to them as they mounted the steep stairs: "Not unless he's come back. I heard him go out at just after eight this morning."

At the top there was a door to the left and a door to the right. Burden knocked on the right one, and it was so rapidly opened that it was apparent Leilie Somers had been listening behind it. And she wanted them inside the flat just as fast. Her neighbour was steadily coming up the stairs and Leilie knew better than to let her hear the law introducing itself or see warrant cards flashed. She was a thin little person of twenty-eight or nine with a pinched face and hennaed hair. Throughout her whole youth she had been the mistress of a man who lived by robbery and occasionally by violent crime, and she had herself been in the dock. But she had never come to adopt, as other women adopt, an attitude of insolence or truculence towards the police. She was always polite, she was always timid, and now as Wexford said, "So you've moved back to your old stamping ground, Leilie," she only nodded and smiled nervously and said yes, that was right, she'd moved back, managed to get this flat which was a piece of luck.

"And Paddy with you, I gather."

"Sometimes," she said. "On and off. He's not what you'd call *living* here."

"What would I call it then? Staying here for his holidays?" Leilie made no answer. The flat seemed to consist of a living room, a bedroom, a lavatory and a kitchen with covered bath in it. They went through to the living room. The furniture in it was ugly and cheap and old but it was very clean and the woodwork and walls were fresh white. The room had been re-decorated perhaps only the week before. There was still a lingering smell of paint. "He was here last night," said Wexford. "He went out around eight this morning. When's he coming back?"

She would be rid of the man if she could be. Wexford had that impression now as he had received it from her once before, years before. Some bond she couldn't break bound her to Paddy Jasper, love or merely habit, but she would be relieved if external circumstances could sever it. Meanwhile, she would be unremittingly loyal.

"What did you want to see him for?"

Two can play at that game, thought Wexford, answering questions with another question. "Where was he last evening?"

"He was here. He had a couple of pals in playing cards and for a beer."

"I don't suppose," said Burden, "that one of these pals was by any chance his little brother Tony?"

Leilie looked at the rug on the floor, up at the ceiling, then out of the window so intently that it seemed there must be at least Concorde manifesting itself up in the sky if not a flying saucer.

"Come on, Leilie, you know Tony. That nice clean-living young Englishman who did two years for mugging an old lady up in the Smoke."

She said very quietly, now staring down at her fingers, "'Course I know Tony. I reckon he was here too, I don't know, I was out at my job." Her voice went up a bit and her chin went up. "I've got an evening job down the Andromeda. Cloakroom attendant, eight till midnight."

A sign of the times, was what Wexford called the Andromeda. It was Kingsmarkham's casino, a gambling club in a spruced-up Victorian house out on the Sewingbury Road. He was going to ask why an evening job, what had happened to her full-time work—for at the time of his last encounter with Leilie she had been a stylist at Mr. Nicholas, the hairdresser's—when his eye fixed itself on an object which stood on one end of the mantelpiece. It was a baby's feeding bottle with dregs of milk still in it.

"I didn't know you had a baby, Leilie," he said.

"He's in the bedroom," she said, and as if to confirm her words there sounded through the wall a reedy wail which quickly gained in volume. She listened. As the cries grew shrill she smiled and the smile became a laugh, a burst of laughter. Then she bit her lip and said in her usual monotone, "Paddy and them were here babysitting for me. They were here all evening."

"I see," said Wexford. He knew then beyond a doubt

that Paddy Jasper had not been there, that his friends had not been there, but that on the other hand they, or some of them including Jasper and his brother, had been up in Ploughman's Lane robbing Baron's Keep. "I see," he said again. The baby went on crying, working itself up into a passion of rage or misery. "Is Paddy the child's father?"

She came the nearest to rudeness she ever had. "You've no right to ask me that, Mr. Wexford. What's it to you?"

No, maybe he had no right, he thought. That ninety-nine out of a hundred policemen would have asked it was no reason why he should. "It's nothing to me," he said. "I'm sorry, Leilie. You'd better go and see to him, hadn't you?"

But at that moment the crying stopped. Leilie Somers sighed. In the flat next door footsteps sounded and a door slammed. Wexford said, "We'll be back," and followed Leilie out into the passage. She went into the bedroom and shut herself in.

Burden let them out and closed the front door. "That's her second child, you know," he said as they went down the stairs. "She had a kid by Jasper years ago."

"Yes, I remember." Wexford recalled Father Glanville's implied admonition and said carefully, "Where is he or she now?"

"She's a baby batterer, is Leilie Somers. Didn't you know? No, you wouldn't. The case came up when you were ill and had all that time off." Wexford didn't much like hearing his month's convalescence after a thrombosis described as "all that time off" but he said nothing. "I was amazed," said Burden severely, "to hear you apologising to her as if she were a decent respectable sort of woman. She's a woman who's capable of giving a helpless baby a fractured skull and a broken arm. Those were her kid's injuries. And what did Leilie get? A suspended sentence, a recommendation for psychiatric treatment, all the nonsense."

"What happened to the little boy?"

"He was adopted," said Burden. "He was quite a long time in hospital and then I heard that Leilie had agreed to have him adopted. Best thing for him."

Wexford nodded. "Strange, though," he said. "She always seems such a gentle meek creature. I can imagine her not knowing how to cope with a child or being a bit too easy-going or not noticing it was ill, say, but baby-battering—it seems so out of character."

"You're always saying how inconsistent people are. You're always saying people are peculiar and you never can tell what they'll do next."

"I suppose I am," said Wexford.

He sent Loring to keep the Roland Road flat under observation, and then he and Burden went to lunch in the police station canteen. Polly Davies came up to Wexford while he was eating his dessert.

"I looked in at Bystall Lane, sir, and saw young Ginger. They said, did we think of making other arrangements for him or were they to keep him for a bit?"

"My God, they haven't had him twenty-four hours yet."

"That's what I said, sir. Well, I sort of said that. I think they're short-staffed."

"So are we," said Wexford. "Now then, I don't suppose anyone saw Karen Bond being put on that doorstep?"

"I'm afraid not, sir. No one I've spoken to, anyway, and no one's come forward. Mrs. Bream who housekeeps for the priest, she says the cardboard box—the Smith's Crisps box, you know—was there when she came at nine only she didn't look at it. She thought it was something someone had left for the father and she was going to take it in once she'd got the kitchen cleared up and his bed made. Father Glanville says he went out at ten to nine and he's positive the box wasn't there then, so someone must have put it there in those ten minutes. It looks like someone who knows their habits, the father's and Mrs. Bream's, doesn't it, sir?"

"One of his flock, d'you mean?"

"It could be. Why not?"

"If you're right," said Wexford dryly, "whoever it was is probably confessing it at this moment and Father Glanville will, of course, have to keep her identity locked in his bosom."

He went off up to his office to await word from Loring. There, sitting at his desk, thinking, he remembered noticing in Susan Rains's flat, honoured on a little shelf fixed there for the purpose, a plaster statuette of the Virgin with lilies in her arms. The Leightons were perhaps a Catholic family. He was on the point of deciding to go back to Greenhill Court for a further talk with Susan Rains when a phone call from Sergeant Camb announced the arrival of Stephen Pollard.

The stockbroker and his wife had been on holiday in Scotland and had driven all the way back, non-stop, all five hundred and forty miles, starting at six that morning. Wexford had met Pollard once before and remembered him as a choleric person. Now he was tired from the long drive but he still rampaged and shouted with as much misery as Pippa Bond had shown over the loss of her baby. The safe, it appeared, had contained a sapphire and platinum necklace and bracelet, four rings, three cameos and a diamond cross which Pollard said were worth thirty thousand pounds. No, of course no one knew he had a safe in which he kept valuables. Well, he supposed the cleaning woman did and the cleaning woman before her

and all of the series of *au pair* girls, and maybe the builders who had painted the outside of the house, and the
firm who had put up the bars.

"It's ludicrous," said Burden when he had gone. "All
that carry-on when it's a dead cert his insurance company'll fork out. He might as well go straight back to
Scotland. We're the people who've got the slog and we'll
get stick if those villains aren't caught, while it won't
make a scrap of difference to him one way or the other.
And I'll tell you another thing that's ludicrous," he said,
warming to a resentful theme. "The ratepayers of Sussex
could have the expense of young Ginger's upbringing for
eighteen years because his mother's too scared to come
and claim him."

"What shall I do about it? Hold a young wives' meeting and draw them a chalk circle?"

Burden looked bewildered.

"Haven't you ever heard of the Chinese chalk circle
and Brecht's *Caucasian Chalk Circle?* You have to draw a
circle in chalk on the ground and put the child in it, and
of the mothers who claim him the one who can pull him
out of the circle is his true mother and may have him."

"That's all very well," said Burden after a pause, "but
in this case, it's not mothers who want him, it's he who
wants a mother. No one seems to want him."

"Poor Ginger," said Wexford, and then the phone rang.
It was Loring on his radio to say Paddy Jasper had come
into Roland Road and gone up the stairs to Leilie
Somers's flat.

--------------◄◆►--------------

By the time Wexford and Burden got there Tony Jasper
had arrived as well. The brothers were both tall, heavily
built men but Tony's figure still had a youthfully athletic

look about it while Paddy had the beginnings of a paunch. Tony's otherwise handsome appearance was ruined by a broken nose which had never been put right and through which he had difficulty in breathing. The repulsive and even sinister air he had was partly due to his always breathing through his mouth. Paddy and he were sitting facing each other at Leilie's living-room table. They were both smoking, the air in the room was thick with smoke, and Tony was dealing a pack of cards. Wexford thought the cards were the inspiration of the moment, hastily fetched out when they heard the knock at the downstairs door.

"Put the cards away, Tone," said Paddy. "It's rude to play when we've got company." He was always polite in a thoroughly offensive way. "Leilie here," he said, "has got something in her head about you wanting to know where I was last evening. Like what sort of time did you have in mind?"

Wexford told him. Paddy smiled. Somehow he managed to make it a paternal smile. He was stopping a few days with Leilie, he said, and his son. He hadn't seen much of his son since the child was born on account of having this good job up north but not a chance of accommodation for a woman and a kid, no way. So he'd come down for his holidays the previous Saturday and what does he hear but that Leilie's got this evening job up the Andromeda. Well, she'd taken Monday night off to be with him and done an exchange with another girl for Tuesday, but when it got to last night she couldn't very well skive off again so he said not to worry, he'd babysit, him and Tony here, and they'd have some of their old mates round. Johnny Farrow and Pip Monkton, for a beer and a hand of solo.

"Which is what we did, Mr. Wexford."

"Right," said Tony.

"Leilie put Matthew in his cot and then the boys came round and she got us a bite to eat. She's a good girl is Leilie. She went off to work about half seven, didn't you, love? Then we did the dishes and had our game. Oh, and the lady next door came round to check up if four grown men could look after baby OK, very kind of her, I'm sure. And then at half eleven Pip went off home on account of his missus being the boss round his place, and at quarter past twelve Leilie came back. She got a lift so she was early. That's right, isn't it, love?"

Leilie nodded. "Except you never did no dishes."

Wexford kept looking at the man's huge feet which were no longer under the table but splayed out across the cheap bright bit of carpet. He wondered where the shoes were that had made those prints. Burnt, probably. The remains of the safe, once they had blown it open, might be in any pond or river in the Home Counties. Johnny Farrow was a notorious peterman or expert with explosives. He turned to Leilie and asked a question perhaps none of them had expected.

"Who usually looks after the baby when you're working?"

"Julie next door. That girl you were talking to when you came earlier. I used to take him to my mum, my mum lives up Charteris Road, it's not very far, but he started getting funny in the evenings, crying and screaming, and he got worse if I took him out and left him in a strange place." Wexford wondered if she was giving him such a detailed answer to his question because she sometimes left the baby unattended and thought she might be breaking the law. He remembered the other boy, the one with the fractured skull and broken arm, and he hardened towards her. "Then Mum had to go into hospital, anyway, she only came out yesterday. So Julie said to leave him here and she'd pop in every half hour, and she'd hear him anyway if he cried. You can hear a pin drop through these walls. And Julie never goes out on account of she's got a baby of her own. She's been very good has Julie because I reckon Matthew does cry most evenings, and you can't just leave them to cry, can you?"

"I'm glad to inform you, my dear," said Paddy with outrageous pomposity, "that my son did not utter a squeak last evening but was as good as gold," and on the last word he looked hard at Wexford and stretched his lips into a huge humourless smile.

———◆———

Julie Lang confirmed that Paddy Jasper, Tony Jasper, Pip Monkton and Johnny Farrow had all been in the flat next door when she called to check on the safety and comfort of Matthew at eight-thirty. She had a key to Leilie's flat but she hadn't used it, knowing Mr. Jasper to be there. She wouldn't have dreamt of doing that because it was Mr. Jasper's home really, wasn't it? So she had knocked at the door and Mr. Jasper had let her in and not been very nice about it actually, and she had felt very awkward especially when he'd said, go in and see for yourself if I'm not to be trusted to look after my own child. He had opened the bedroom door and made her look and she had just glanced at the cot and seen Matthew was all right and sleeping.

"Well, I felt so bad about it," said Julie Lang, "that I said to him, perhaps he'd like the key back, and he said, yes, he'd been going to ask me for it as they wouldn't be needing my services any longer, thanks very much. He was quite rude really but I did feel bad about it."

She had given Paddy Jasper the key. As far as she

knew, the four men had remained in the flat with Matthew till Leilie got back at twelve-fifteen. By then, anyway, her husband had come home and they were both in bed asleep. No, she had heard no footsteps on the stairs, not even those of Pip Monkton going home at eleven-thirty. Of course she had had the television on so maybe she wouldn't have heard, but she was positive there hadn't been a sound out of Matthew.

Wexford and Burden went next to the home of Pip Monkton. Johnny Farrow's confirmation of the alibi would amount to very little, for he had a long criminal record for safebreaking, but Monkton had never been convicted of anything, had never even been charged with anything. He was an ex-publican, apparently perfectly respectable, and the only blot on his white innocent life was his known friendship with Farrow with whom he had been at school and whom he had supported and stuck to during Farrow's long prison sentences and periods of poverty-stricken idleness. If Monkton said that the four of them had been together all that evening babysitting in Leilie Somers's flat, Wexford knew he might as well throw up the sponge. The judge, the jury, the court, would believe Pip Monkton just as they would believe Julie Lang.

And Monkton did say it. Looking Wexford straight in the eye (so that the chief inspector knew he must be lying) he declared boldly that he and the Jaspers and Johnny had been in Roland Road, playing solo and drinking beer, until he left for home at half-past eleven. Wexford had him down to the police station and went on asking him about it, but he couldn't break him down. Monkton sounded as if he had learnt by heart what he had to say, and he went on saying it over and over again like a talking bird or a record on which the needle has got stuck.

When it got to six Wexford had himself driven to the Andromeda where the manager, who had an interest in keeping on the right side of the police, answered his questions very promptly. He got back to the station to find Burden and Polly discussing the one relevant piece of information Burden had succeeded in finding out about Monkton—that he had recently had an extension built on to his house. To cover the cost of this he had taken out a second mortgage, but the costs had come to three thousand pounds more than the builder's estimate.

"That'll be about what Monkton's getting for perjury," said Burden. "That'll be his share. Tony drove the van, Paddy and Johnny did the job while Monkton covers for them. I imagine they left Leilie's place around nine and got to Ploughman's Lane by a quarter past. They'll have got the safe out in an hour and got to the gate in the fence with it by ten-thirty, which was just about the time Willoughby spotted the van. Tony drove off, ditched the van in Myringham, came back to Stowerton on the last bus, the one that leaves Myringham at ten past eleven and which would have got him to Stowerton High Street by ten to twelve. God knows how the others got that safe back. My guess is that they didn't. They hid it in one of the meadows at the back of Ploughman's Lane and went back for it this morning—with Johnny Farrow's car. Then Johnny blew it. They used the wheels again and Johnny blew it somewhere up on the downs."

Wexford hadn't spoken for some minutes. Now he said, "When Leilie Somers was charged with this baby-battering thing, did she plead guilty or not guilty?"

Rather surprised by the apparent irrelevance of this question, Burden said, "Guilty. There wasn't much evidence offered apart from the doctor's. Leilie pleaded guilty and said something about being tired and strained and not being able to stand it when the baby cried. Damned disgraceful nonsense."

"Yes, it was damned disgraceful nonsense," said Wexford quietly, and then he said, "The walls in those flats are very thin, aren't they? So thin that from one side you can hear a pin drop on the other." He was silent and meditative for a moment. "What was Leilie Somers's mother's maiden name?"

"*What?*" said Burden. "How on earth do you expect me to know a thing like that?"

"I just thought you might. I thought it might be an Irish name, you see. Because Leilie is probably short for Eileen, which is an Irish name. I expect she called herself Leilie when she was too young to pronounce her name properly."

Burden said with an edge of impatience to his voice, "Look, do I get to know what all this is leading up to?"

"Sure you do. The arrest of Paddy and Tony Jasper and Johnny Farrow. You can get down to Roland Road and see to it as soon as you like."

"For God's sake, you know as well as I do we'll never make it stick. We couldn't break Monkton and he'll alibi the lot of them."

"That'll be OK," said Wexford laconically. "Trust me. Believe me, there is no alibi. And now, Polly, you and I will turn our attention to the matter of young Ginger and the Kingsmarkham Chalk Circle."

————◆————

Wexford left Polly sitting outside in the car. It was eight o'clock and still light. He rang the bell that had fetched Leilie down that afternoon, and when she didn't come he rang the other. Julie Lang appeared.

"She's upset. I've got her in with me having a cup of tea."

"I'd like to see her, Mrs. Lang, and I'll need to see her alone. I'll go and sit in my car for five minutes and then if she'll . . ."

Leilie Somers's voice from the top of the stairs cut off the end of his sentence. "You can come up. I'm OK now."

Wexford climbed the stairs towards her, Julie Lang following him. Leilie stood back to let him pass. She seemed smaller than ever, thinner, meeker, her hennaed hair showing a paler red at the roots, her face white and deeply sad. Julie Lang put her hand on her arm, squeezed it, went off quickly into her own flat. Leilie put the key into the lock of her front door and opened the door and stood looking at the empty neat place, the passage, the open doors into the other rooms, now all made more melancholy by the encroaching twilight. Tears stood in her eyes and she turned her face so that Wexford should not see them fall.

"He's not worth it, Leilie," said Wexford.

"I know *that*, I know what he's worth. But you won't get me being disloyal to him, Mr. Wexford, I shan't say a word."

"Let's go in and sit down." He made his way to the table where it was lightest and sat down in the chair Tony Jasper had sat in. "Where's the baby?"

"With my mum."

"Rather much for someone who's just come out of hospital, isn't it?" Wexford looked at his watch. "You're going to be late for work. What time is it you start? Eight-thirty?"

"Eight," she said. "I'm not going. I couldn't, not after what's happened to Paddy. Mr. Wexford, you might as well go. I'm not going to say anything. If I was Paddy's wife you couldn't make me say anything, and I'm as good as his wife, I've been more to him than most wives'd have been."

"I know that, Leilie," said Wexford, "I know all about that," and his voice was so loaded with meaning that she stared at him with frightened eyes whose whites shone in the dusk. "Leilie," he said, "when they drew the chalk circle and put·the child in it the girl who had brought him up refused to pull him out because she knew she would hurt him. Rather than hurt him she preferred that some- one else should have him."

"I don't know what you're talking about," she said.

"I think you do. It's not so different from Solomon's judgement of cutting the baby in half. The child's mother wouldn't have that happen, better let the other woman have him. You pleaded guilty in court to crimes against your first son you had never committed. It was Jasper who injured that child, and it was Jasper who got you to take the blame because he knew you would get a light sentence whereas he would get a heavy one. And after- wards you had the baby adopted—not because you didn't love him but because like the chalk circle woman you would rather lose him than have him hurt again. Isn't it true?"

She stared at him. Her head moved, a tiny affirmative bob. Wexford leaned across to the window and opened it. He waved his hand out of the window, withdrew it and closed the casement again. Leilie was crying, making no attempt to dry her tears.

"Were you brought up as a Catholic?" he said.

"I was baptized," she said in a voice not much above a whisper. "Mum's a Catholic. Her and Dad, they got mar- ried in Galway where Mum comes from, and Dad had to promise to bring the kids up Catholic." A sob caught her throat. "I haven't been to mass for years. Mr. Wexford, please go away now and leave me alone. I just want to be left alone."

He said, "I'm sorry to hear you say that because I've

got a visitor for you, and he'll certainly be staying the
night." He switched on lights, the living-room light, the
light in the hall and one over the top of the door, and
then he opened the door and Polly Davies walked in with
young Ginger in her arms.

Leilie blinked at the light. She closed her eyes and low-
ered her head, and then she lifted it and opened her eyes
and made a sort of bound for Polly, nearly knocking Wexford over. But she didn't snatch Ginger. She stood trembling, looking at Polly, her hands moving slowly forward
until, with an extreme gentle tenderness, they closed over
and caressed the baby's downy red-gold head.

"Matthew," she said. "Matthew."

———————◄◆►———————

The baby lay in Leilie's lap. He had whimpered a little at
first, but now he lay quiet and relaxed, gripping one of
her fingers, and for the first time in their acquaintance
Wexford saw him smile. It was a beautiful spontaneous
smile of happiness at being home again with Mother.

"You're going to tell me all about it, aren't you, Leilie?"
said Wexford.

She was transformed. He had never seen her so ani-
mated, so high-spirited. She was giggly with joy so that
Matthew, sensing her mood, gurgled in response, and she
hugged him again, calling him her lovely lovely sweet-
heart, her precious boy.

"Come on now, Leilie," said Wexford, "you've got him
back without the least trouble to yourself which is more
than you damn' well deserve. Now you can give an account of yourself."

"I don't know where to start," said Leilie, giggling.

"At the beginning, whenever that is."

"Well, the beginning," said Leilie, "I reckon when Patrick, my first boy, was adopted." She had stopped laugh-

ing and a little of the old melancholy had come back into
her face. "That was four years ago. Paddy went off up
north and after a bit he wrote and said would I join him,
and I don't know why I said yes, I reckon I always do say
yes to Paddy, and there didn't seem anything else, there
didn't seem any future. It was all right with Paddy for a
bit, and then a couple of years back he got this other girl.
I sort of pretended I didn't know about it, I thought he'd
get tired of her, but he didn't and I was lonely, I was so
lonely. I didn't know a soul up there but Paddy, not like I
could talk to, and he'd go away for weeks on end. I sort of
took to going out with other fellas, anyone, I didn't care,
just for the company." She paused, shifted Matthew on
her knees. "When I knew I was pregnant I told Paddy I
wasn't having the baby up there, I was going home to
Mum. But he said to stay and he wouldn't see the other
girl, and I did stay till after Matthew was born, and then
I knew he was carrying on again so I came back here and
Mum got me this flat. I know what you're going to say,
Mr. Wexford!"

"I wasn't going to say a word."

"You were thinking it. So what? It's true. I couldn't tell
you who Matthew's father is, I don't know. It might be
Paddy, it might be one of half a dozen." Her expression
had grown fierce. She almost glared at him. "And I'm
glad I don't know. I'm glad. It makes him more mine. I
never went out with any other fella but Paddy till he
drove me to it."

"All right," said Wexford, "all right. So you lived here
with Matthew and you had your job at the Andromeda
and then Paddy wrote to say he was coming down, and
on Saturday he did come. And you took Monday evening
off work to be with him and exchanged your Tuesday
turn with another girl—and so we come to Wednesday,
yesterday."

Leilie sighed. She didn't seem unhappy, only rueful. "Paddy said he'd babysit. He said he'd asked Tony over and Johnny and a fella called Pip Monkton, and they'd be in all evening. I said he wasn't to bother, I could take Matthew next door into Julie's, and Paddy got mad at me and said Julie was an interfering bitch and didn't I trust him to look after his own child? Well, that was it, I didn't, I kept remembering what he'd done to Patrick, and that was because Patrick cried. Paddy used to go crazy when he cried, I used to think he'd kill him, and when I tried to stop him he nearly killed me. And, you see, Mr. Wexford, Matthew'd got into this way of crying in the evenings. They said at the clinic some babies cry at night and some in the evenings and it's hard to know why, but they all grow out of it. I knew Matthew'd start screaming about eight and I thought, my God, what'll Paddy do? He gets in a rage, he doesn't know what he's doing, and Tony wouldn't stop him, he's scared of him like they all are, Paddy's so big. Well, I got in a real state. Mum'd come out of hospital that morning, she'd had a major op, so I couldn't take him there and go back there myself and hide from Paddy, and I couldn't take him to work. I did once and they made a hell of a fuss. I just couldn't see any way out of it.

"Paddy went out about eleven. He never said where he was going and I didn't ask. Anyway, I went out too, carrying Matthew in the baby carrier, and I just walked about thinking. I reckon I must have walked miles, worrying about it and wondering what to do and imagining all sorts of things, you know how you do. I'd been feeding Matthew myself and I'm still giving him one feed a day, so I took him into a field and fed him under a hedge, and after that I walked a bit more.

"Well, I was coming back along the Stowerton Road. I

knew I'd have to go home on account of Matthew was wet and he'd soon be hungry again, and then I saw this pram. I knew who it belonged to, I'd seen it there before and I'd seen this girl lift her baby out of it. I mean, I didn't know her name or anything but I'd talked to her once queueing for the check-out in the Tesco, and we'd got talking about our babies and she said hers never cried except sometimes for a feed in the night. She was such a good baby, they never got a peep out of her all day and all evening. She was a bit younger than Matthew but it was funny, they looked a bit alike and they'd got just the same colour hair.

"That was what gave me the idea, them having the same colour hair. I know I was mad, Mr. Wexford, I know that now. I was crazy, but you don't know how scared of Paddy I was. I went over to that pram and I bent over it. I unhooked the cat net and took the other baby out and put Matthew in."

Until now quite silent in her corner, Polly Davies gave a suppressed exclamation. Wexford drew in his breath, shaking his head.

"It's interesting," he said, and his voice was frosty, "how I supposed at first that whoever had taken Karen Bond wanted her and wished to be rid of her own child. Now it looks as if the reverse was true. It looks as if she didn't at all mind sacrificing Karen for her own child's safety."

Leilie said passionately, "That's not true!"

"No, perhaps it isn't, I believe you did have second thoughts. Go on."

"I put Matthew in the pram. I knew he'd be all right. I knew no one'd hurt him, but it went to my heart when he started to cry."

"Weren't you afraid someone would see you?" asked Polly.

"I wouldn't have cared if they had. Don't you see? I was past caring for any of that. If I'd been seen I wouldn't have had to go home, I'd have lost my job, but they wouldn't have taken Matthew from me, would they? No one saw me. Did you say her name was Karen? Well, I took Karen home and I fed her and bathed her. No one can say I didn't look after her like she was my own."

"Except for delivering her into the hands of that ravening wolf, Paddy Jasper," said Wexford unpleasantly.

She shivered a little but otherwise she took no notice. "Paddy came in at six with Tony. The baby was in Matthew's cot by then. All you could see was its red hair like Matthew's. I remembered what that girl had said about her never crying in the evenings, and I thought, I prayed, don't cry tonight, don't cry because you're in a strange place." Leilie lifted her head and began to speak more rapidly. "I cooked egg and chips for the lot of them and I went out at half seven. I got back at a quarter past twelve and she was OK, she was fast asleep and she hadn't cried at all."

Wexford said softly, "Haven't you forgotten something, Leilie?"

Her eyes darted over him. He fancied she had grown a little paler. She picked up Matthew and held him closely against her. "Well, the next day," she said. "Today. Paddy went off out early so I thought about getting the baby back. I thought of taking her to the priest. I knew about the priest, when he went out and when the lady cleaner came, I knew about it from Mum. So I got on the bus to Kingsmarkham and just by the bus stop's a shop where they'd put all their boxes out on the pavement for the dustmen. I took a box and put the baby in and left her on the doorstep of the priest's house. But I didn't know how I was going to get Matthew back, I thought I'd never get him back.

"And then you came. I said Matthew was in the bedroom and just then Julie's baby started crying and you thought it was Matthew. I couldn't help laughing, though I felt I was going to pieces, I was being torn apart. And that's all, that's everything, and now you can charge me with whatever it is I've done."

"But you've forgotten something, Leilie."

"I don't know what you mean," she said.

"Of course you do. Why d'you think I had Paddy and Tony and Johnny Farrow arrested even though Pip Monkton had given them all a cast-iron alibi? How do you think I know Pip will break down and tell me that tale of his was all moonshine and tell me as well just where the contents of that safe are now? I had a little talk with the management of the Andromeda this afternoon, Leilie."

She gave him a stony stare.

"You've got the sack, haven't you?" he said. "Work out your notice till the end of next week or go now. They were bound to catch you out."

"If you know all about it, Mr. Wexford, why ask?"

"Because I want you to say yes."

She whispered something to the baby, but the baby had fallen asleep.

"If you won't tell me, I shall tell you," said Wexford, "and if I get it wrong you can stop me. I'm going to tell you about those second thoughts you had, Leilie. You went off to work like you said but you weren't easy in your mind. You kept thinking about that baby, that other baby, that good baby that never cried in the evenings. But maybe the reason she didn't cry was that she was usually in her own bed, safe and secure in her own home with her own mother, maybe it'd be different if she woke up to find herself in a strange place. So you started worrying. You ran around that glorified ladies' loo where you work, wiping the basins and filling the towel machines and taking your ten pence tips, but you were going off your head with worry about that other baby. You kept thinking of her crying and what that animal Paddy Jasper might do to her if she cried, punch her with his great fists perhaps or bash her head against the wall. And then you knew you hadn't done anything so clever after all in swapping Matthew for her, because you're a kind loving woman at heart, Leilie, though you're a fool, and you were as worried about her as you'd have been about him."

"And you're a devil," whispered Leilie, staring at him as if he had supernatural powers. "How d'you know what I thought?"

"I just know," said Wexford. "I know what you thought and I know what you did. When it got to half-past nine you couldn't stand it any longer. You put on your coat and ran out to catch the nine-thirty-five bus and you were home, walking up those stairs, by five to ten. There were lights on in the flat. You let yourself in and went straight into the bedroom, and Karen was in there, safe and sound and fast asleep."

Leilie smiled a little. A ghost of a smile of happy recollection crossed her face and was gone. "I don't know how you know," she said, "but yes, she was OK and asleep, and oh God, the relief of it. I'd been picturing her lying there with blood on her and I don't know what."

"So all you had to do then was explain to Paddy why you'd come home."

"I told him I felt ill," said Leilie carefully. "I said I felt rotten and I'd got one of my migraines coming."

"No, you didn't. He wasn't there."

"What d'you mean, wasn't there? He was there! Him and Tony and Pip and Johnny, they were in here playing cards. I said to Paddy, I feel rotten, I had to come home.

I'm going to have a lay-down, I said, and I went into the bedroom and laid down."

"Leilie, when you came in the flat was empty. You know it was empty. You know Pip Monkton's lying and you know his story won't stand up for two seconds once you tell the truth that at *five to ten this flat was empty.* Listen to me, Leilie. Paddy will go away for quite a long time over this business. It'll be a chance for you and young Ginge—er, Matthew, to make a new life. You don't want him round you for ever, do you? Ruining your life, beating up your kids? Do you, Leilie?"

She lifted the baby in her arms. She walked the length of the room and half back again as if he were restless and needed soothing instead of peacefully asleep. In front of Wexford she stood still, looking at him, and he got to his feet.

"We'll come and fetch you in the morning, Leilie," he said, "and take you to the police station where I'll want you to make a statement. Maybe two statements. One about taking Karen and one about Paddy not being here when you came back last night."

"I won't say a thing about that," she said.

"It might be that we wouldn't proceed with any charge against you for taking Karen."

"I don't care about that!"

He hated doing it. He knew he had to. "A woman who knew what you knew about Paddy and who still exposed a child to him, someone else's child—how'll that sound in court, Leilie? When they know you're living with Paddy again? And when they hear your record?"

Her face had gone white and she clasped Matthew against her. "They wouldn't take him away from me? They wouldn't make a what-d'you-call-it?"

"A care order? They might."

"Oh God, oh God. I promised myself I'd stick by Paddy all my life. . . ."

"Romantic promises, Leilie, they haven't much to do with real life." Wexford moved a little away from her. He went to the window. It was quite dark outside now. "They told me at the Andromeda that you came back at half-past ten. You'd been away an hour and there had been complaints so they sacked you."

She said feverishly, "I did go back. I told Paddy I felt better, I . . ."

"All in the space of five minutes? Or ten at the most? You were quickly ill and well, Leilie. Shall I tell you why you went back, shall I tell you the only circumstances in which you'd have dared go back? You didn't want to lose your job but you were more afraid of what Paddy might do to the baby. If Paddy had been there the one thing you wouldn't have done is go back. Because he wasn't there you went back with a light heart. You believed he could only get in again when you were there to let him in. You didn't know then that he had a key, the key he had taken from Julie Lang."

She spoke at last the word he had been waiting for. "Yes." She nodded. "Yes, it's true. If I'd known he had that key," she said, and she shivered, "I'd no more have gone and left that baby there than I'd have left it in the lion house at the zoo."

"We'll be on our way," he said. "Come along, Constable Davies. See you in the morning, Leilie."

Still holding Matthew, she came up to him just as he reached the door and laid a hand on his sleeve. "I've been thinking about what you said, Mr. Wexford," she said, "and I don't think I'd be able to pull anybody's baby, *any* baby, out of that circle."

Achilles Heel

The walls of the city afforded on one side a view of the blue Adriatic, on the other, massed roofs, tiled in weathered terracotta, and cataracts of stone streets descending to the cathedral and the Stradun Placa. It was very hot on the walls, the sun hard and the air dry and clear. Among the red-brown roofs and the complexities of ramparts and stairs, different colours shimmered, the purple of the bougainvillaea, the sky blue of the plumbago, and the flame flash of the orange trumpet flower.

"Lovely," said Dora Wexford. "Breathtaking. Aren't you glad now I made you come up here?"

"It's all right for you dark-skinned people," grumbled her husband. "My nose is beginning to feel like a fried egg."

"We'll go down at the next lot of steps and you can administer some more sun cream over a glass of beer."

It was noon, the date Saturday, 18 June. The full heat of the day had kept the Yugoslavs, but not the tourists, off the walls. Germans went by with cameras or stood, murmuring, "Wunderschön!" Vivacious Italians chattered, unaffected by the midsummer sun. But some of the snatches of talk which reached Wexford were in languages not only incomprehensible but unidentifiable. It was a surprise to hear English spoken.

"Don't keep on about it, Iris!"

At first they couldn't see the speaker. But now, as they

came out of the narrow defile and emerged on to one of the broad jutting courts made by a buttress top, they came face to face with the Englishman. A tall, fair young man, he was standing in the furthest angle of the court, and with him was a dark-haired girl. Her back was to the Wexfords. She was staring out to sea. From her clothes, she looked as if she would have been more at home in the South of France than on the walls of Dubrovnik. She wore a jade-green halter top that left her deeply tanned midriff bare, and a calf-length silk skirt in green and blue with parabolas on it of flamingo pink. Her sandals were pink, the strings criss-crossed up her legs, the wedge heels high. But perhaps the most striking thing about her was her hair. Raven black and very short, it was cut at the nape in three sharp Vs.

She must have replied to her companion, though Wexford hadn't heard the words. But now, without turning round, she stamped her foot and the man said:

"How can you go to the bloody place, Iris, when we can't find anyone to take us? There's nowhere to land. I wish to God you'd give it a rest."

Dora took her husband's arm, hastening him along. He could read her thoughts, not to eavesdrop on someone else's quarrel.

"You're so nosy, darling," she said when they had reached the steps and were out of earshot. "I suppose it's what comes of being a policeman."

Wexford laughed. "I'm glad you realise that's the reason. Any other man's wife would accuse him of looking at that girl."

"She *was* beautiful, wasn't she?" said Dora wistfully, conscious of her age. "Of course we couldn't see her face, but you could tell she had a perfect figure."

"Except for the legs. Pity she hasn't got the sense to wear trousers."

"Oh, Reg, what was wrong with her legs? And she was so beautifully tanned. When I see a girl like that it makes me feel such an old has-been."

"Don't be so daft," said Wexford crossly. "You look fine." He meant it. He was proud of his handsome wife, so young-looking for her late fifties, elegant and decorous in navy skirt and crisp white blouse, her skin already golden after only two days of holiday. "And I'll tell you one thing," he added. "You'd beat her hollow in any ankle competition."

Dora smiled at him, comforted. They sat down at a table in a pavement café where the shade was deep and a cool breeze blew. Just time for a beer and an orange juice, and then to catch the water taxi back down the coast to Mirna.

———◆———

In Serbo-Croat *mirna* means peaceful. And so Wexford found the resort after a gruelling winter and spring in Kingsmarkham, after petty crime and serious crime, and finally a squalid murder case which had been solved, not by him in spite of his work and research, but by a young expert from Scotland Yard. It was Mike Burden who had advised him to get right away for his holiday. Not Wales or Cornwall this time, but the Dalmatian coast of Yugoslavia where he, Burden, had taken his children the previous year.

"Mirna," said Burden. "There are three good hotels but the village is quite unspoilt. You can go everywhere by water. Two or three old chaps run taxi boats. It never rained once while we were there. And you're into all this nature stuff, this ecology. The marine life's amazing and so are the flowers and butterflies."

It was the marine life with which Wexford was getting acquainted two mornings after the trip to Dubrovnik.

He had left Dora prone on an air bed by the hotel swimming pool, knowing full well that sunbathing was impossible for his Anglo-Saxon skin. Already his nose was peeling. So he had anointed his face, put on a long-sleeved
shirt, and walked round the wooded point to Mirna harbour. The little port had a harbour wall built of the same
stone as the city of Dubrovnik, and kneeling down to peer
over, he saw that beneath the water line the rocks and
masonry were thickly covered by a tapestry of sea anemones and tiny shells and flowering weed and starfishes.
The water was perfectly clear and unpolluted. He could
clearly see the bottom, fifteen feet down, and now a shoal
of silvery-brown fish glided out from a sea-bed bush. Fascinated, he leaned over, understanding why so many
swimmers out there were equipped with goggles and
schnorkels. A scarlet fish darted out from a rock, then a
broad silver one, banded with black.

Behind him, a voice said, "You like it?"

Wexford got up on to his haunches. The man who had
spoken was older than he, skinny and wrinkled and
tough-looking. He had a walnut face, a dry smile and surprisingly good teeth. He wore a sailor's cap and a blue
and white striped tee-shirt, and Wexford recognised him
as one of the taxi boatmen.

He replied slowly and carefully, "I like it very much. It
is pretty, beautiful."

"The shores of your country were like this once. But in
the nineteenth century a man called Gosse, a marine biol-
ogist, wrote a book about them and within a few years
collectors had come and divested the rocks of everything."

Wexford couldn't help laughing. "Good God," he said.
"I beg your pardon, but I thought . . ."

"That an old boatman can say 'please' and 'zank you' and 'ten dinara'?"

"Something like that." Wexford got up to stand inches taller than the other man. "You speak remarkable English."

A broad smile. "No, it is too pedantic. I have only once been to England and that many years ago." He put out his hand. "How do you do, *gospodine?* Ivo Racic at your service."

"Reginald Wexford."

The hand was iron hard but the grip gentle. Racic said, "I do not wish to intrude. I spoke to you because it is rare to find a tourist interested in nature. With most it is only the sunbathing and the food and drink, eh? Or to catch the fish and take the shells."

"Come and have a drink," said Wexford, "or are you working?"

"Josip and Mirko and I, we have a little syndicate, and they will not mind if I have a half an hour off. But I buy the drinks. This is my country and you are my guest."

They walked towards the avenue of stout palm trees. "I was born here in Mirna," said Racic. "At eighteen I left for the university and when I retired and came back here after forty years and more, those palm trees were just the same, no bigger, no different. Nothing was changed till they built the hotels."

"What did you do in those forty years? Not run a boat service?"

"I was professor of Anglo-Saxon studies at the University of Beograd, Gospodin Wexford."

"Ah," said Wexford, "all is made plain. And when you retired you took up with Josip and Mirko to run the water taxis. Perhaps they were childhood friends?"

"They were. I see you have perspicacity. And may I enquire in return what is your occupation?"

Wexford said what he always said on holiday, "I'm a civil servant."

Racic smiled. "Here in Yugoslavia we are all civil servants. But let us go for our drinks. *Hajdemo, drug!*"

They chose a cluster of tables set under a vine-covered canopy, through which the sun made a gentle dappling on cobbles. Racic drank *slivovic*. The fiery brandy with its hinted undertaste of plums was forbidden to Wexford who had to watch his blood pressure. He even felt guilty when the white wine called Posip which Racic ordered for him arrived in a tumbler filled to the brim.

"You live here in Mirna?"

"Here alone in my *kucica* that was once my father's house. My wife died in Beograd. But it is a good and pleasant life. I have my pension and my boat and the grapes I grow and the figs, and sometimes a guest like yourself, Gospodin Wexford, on whom to practise my English."

Wexford would have liked to question him about the political regime, but he felt that this might be unwise and perhaps discourteous. So instead he remarked on the stately appearance of a woman in national costume, white coif, heavily embroidered stiff black dress, who had emerged with a full basket from the grocer's shop. Racic nodded, then pointed a brown thumb to a table outside the shadow of the vines.

"That is better, I think. Healthier, eh? And freer."

She was sitting in the full sun, a young woman with short black hair geometrically cut, who wore only a pair of white shorts and jade-green halter top. A man came out of the currency exchange bureau, she got up to meet him, and Wexford recognised them as the couple he had seen on the walls of Dubrovnik. They went off hand in hand and got into a white Lancia Gamma parked under the palms.

"Last time I saw them they were quarrelling."

"They are staying at the Hotel Bosnia," said Racic. "On Sunday evening they drove here from Dubrovnik and they are going to remain for a week. Her name I cannot tell you, but his is Philip."

"May I ask how you come to be such a mine of information, Mr. Racic?"

"They came out in my boat this morning." Racic's dark bright eyes twinkled. "Just the two of them, to be ferried across to Vrt and back. But let me tell you a little story. Once, about a year ago, a young English couple hired my boat. They were, I think, on their wedding journey, their honeymoon, as you say, and it was evident they were much in love. They had no eyes but for each other and certainly no inclination to speak to the boatman. We were coming into the shore here, perhaps a hundred metres out, when the young husband began telling his wife how much he loved her and how he could hardly wait to get back to the hotel to make love to her. Oh, very frank and explicit he was—and why not with only the old Yugoslav there who speaks nothing but his own outlandish tongue?

"I said nothing. I betrayed nothing in my face. We pulled in, he paid me twenty dinars and they walked off up the quay. Then I saw the young lady had left her bag behind and I called to her. She came back, took it and thanked me. Gospodin Wexford, I could not resist it. "You have a charming husband, madame," I said, "but no more than you deserve." Oh, how she blushed, but I think she was not displeased, though they never came in my boat again."

Laughing, Wexford said, "It was hardly a similar conversation you overheard between Philip and his wife, though?"

"No." Racic looked thoughtful. "I think I will not tell you what I overheard. It is no business of ours. And now I must make my excuses, but we shall meet again."

"In your boat, certainly. I must take my wife over to Vrt for the bathing."

"Better than that. Bring your wife and I will take you for a trip round the islands. On Wednesday? No, I'm not touting for custom. This will be a trip—now for a good colloquial expression—on the house! You and me and Gospoda Wexford."

"Those very nice Germans," said Dora, "have asked us to go with them in their car to Cetinje on Wednesday."

"Mm," said Wexford absently. "Good idea." It was nine o'clock but very dark beyond the range of the waterside lights. They had walked into Mirna after dinner, it being too late for the taxi boats, and were having coffee on the terrace of a restaurant at the harbour edge. The nearly tideless Adriatic lapped the stones at their feet with soft gulping sounds.

Suddenly he remembered. "Oh, God, I can't. I promised that Yugoslav I told you about to go on a trip round the islands with him. It'd look discourteous to let him down. But you go to Cetinje."

"Well, I should like to. I may never get another chance to see Montenegro. Oh, look, darling, there are those people we saw in Dubrovnik!"

For the first time Wexford saw the girl full-face. Her haircut from the front was as spectacular as from the back, a fringe having been cut into a sharp peak in the centre of her forehead. It looked less like hair, he thought, than a black cap painted on. In spite of the hour, she wore large tinted glasses. Her coloured skirt was the same one she had been wearing that first time.

She and her companion had come on to the terrace from the harbour walk. They walked slowly, she somehow reluctantly, the man called Philip looking about him as if for friends they had arranged to meet here. It couldn't have been for a vacant table, for the terrace was half-empty. Dora kicked her husband's foot under the table, a warning against overt curiosity, and started to talk about her German friends, Werner and Trudi. Out of the corner of his eye, Wexford saw the man and the girl hesitate, then sit down at a neighbouring table. He made some sort of reply to Dora, conscious that it was he now who was being stared at. A voice he had heard once before said:

"Excuse me, we don't seem to have an ashtray. Would you mind if we had yours?"

Dora handed it to him. "Please do." She hardly looked up.

He insisted, smiling. "You're sure you won't need it?"

"Quite sure. We don't smoke."

He wasn't the kind to give up easily, thought Wexford, and now, very intrigued by something he had noticed, he didn't want to. Another prod from Dora's foot merely made him withdraw his own under his chair. He turned towards the other table, and to the next question, "Are you staying long in Mirna?" he replied pleasantly, "A fortnight. We've been here four days."

The effect of this simple rejoinder was startling. The man couldn't have expressed more satisfaction—and, yes, relief—if Wexford had brought him news of some great inheritance or that a close friend, presumed in danger, was safe.

"Oh, fantastic! That's really great. It's such a change to meet some English people. We must try and get together. This is my wife. We're called Philip and Iris Nyman. Are you Londoners too?"

Wexford introduced himself and Dora and said that they were from Kingsmarkham in Sussex. It was lovely to meet them, said Philip Nyman. They must let him buy them a drink. No? More coffee, then? At last Wexford accepted a cup of coffee, wondering what was so upsetting Iris Nyman that she had responded to the introduction only with a nod and now seemed almost paralysed. Her husband's extrovert behaviour? Certainly his effusive manner would have embarrassed all but the most insensitive. As soon as they had settled the question of the drinks, he launched into a long account of their trip from England, how they had come down through France and Italy, the people they had met, the weather, their delight at their first sight of the Dalmatian coast which they had never previously visited. Iris Nyman showed no delight. She simply stared out to sea, gulping down *slivovic* as if it were lemonade.

"We absolutely adored it. They say it's the least spoilt of the Mediterranean resorts, and that I can believe. We all loved Dubrovnik. That is, I mean, we brought a cousin of my wife's along with us. She was going on to holiday with some people she knows in Greece, so she flew to Athens from Dubrovnik on Sunday and left us to come on here."

Dora said, "We saw you in Dubrovnik. On the walls."

Iris Nyman's glass made a little clinking sound against her teeth. Her husband said, "You saw us on the walls? D'you know, I think I remember that." He seemed just slightly taken aback. But not deterred. "In fact, I seem to remember we were having a bit of a row at the time."

Dora made a deprecating movement with her hands. "We just walked past you. It was terribly hot, wasn't it?"

"You're being very charmingly discreet, Mrs. Wexford —or may I call you Dora? The point was, Dora, my wife wanted to climb one of the local mountains and I was telling her just how impractical this was. I mean, in that heat, and for what? To get the same view you get from the walls."

"So you managed to dissuade her?" Wexford said quietly.

"Indeed I did, but you came along rather at the height of the ding-dong. Another drink, darling? And how about you, Dora? Won't you change your mind?"

They replied simultaneously, "Another *slivovic*," and "Thank you so much, but we must go." It was a long time since Wexford had seen his wife so huffy and so thoroughly out of countenance. He marvelled at Nyman's continuing efforts, his fixed smile.

"Let me guess, you're staying at the Adriatic?" He took silence for assent. "We're at the Bosnia. Wait a minute, how about making a date for, say, Wednesday? We could all have a trip somewhere in my car."

The Wexfords, having previous engagements, were able to refuse with clear consciences. They said good night, Wexford nodding non-committally at Nyman's insistence that they must meet again, mustn't lose touch after having been so lucky as to encounter each other. His eyes followed them. Wexford looked back once to see.

"Well!" said Dora when they were out of earshot, "what an insufferably rude woman!"

"Just very nervous, I think," said Wexford thoughtfully. He gave her his arm and they began the walk back along the waterside path. It was very dark, the sea inky and calm, the island invisible. "When you come to think of it, that was all very odd."

"Was it? She was rude and he was effusive to the point of impertinence, if you call that odd. He forced himself on us, got us to tell him our names—you could see she just didn't want to know. I was amazed when he called me Dora."

"That part wasn't so odd. After all, that's how one does make holiday acquaintances. Presumably it was much the same with Werner and Trudi."

"No, it wasn't, Reg, not at all. For one thing, we're much of an age and we're staying at the same hotel. Trudi speaks quite good English, and we were watching the children in the paddling pool and she happened to mention her grandsons who are just the same age as ours, and that started it. You must see that's quite different from a man of thirty walking into a café and latching on to a couple old enough to be his parents. I call it pushy."

Wexford reacted impatiently. "That's as may be. Perhaps you didn't notice there was a perfectly clean ashtray in the middle of that table before they sat down at it."

"*What?*" Dora halted, staring at him in the dark.

"There was. He must have put it in his pocket to give him an excuse for speaking to us. Now that was odd. And giving us all that gratuitous information was odd. And telling a deliberate lie was very odd indeed. Come along, my dear. Don't stand there gawping at me."

"What do you mean, a deliberate lie?"

"When you told them we'd seen them on the walls, he said he remembered it and we must have overheard the quarrel between himself and his wife. Now that was odd in itself. Why mention it at all? Why should we care about his domestic—or maybe I should say mural—rows? He said the quarrel had been over climbing a mountain, but no one climbs the mountains here in summer. Besides, I remember precisely what he did say up on the walls. He said, 'We can't find anyone to take us.' OK, so he might have meant they couldn't get a guide. But 'there's nowhere to land?' That's what he said, no doubt about it. You don't land on mountains, Dora, unless you assault them by helicopter."

"I wonder why, though? I wonder what he's up to?"

"So do I," said Wexford, "but I'm pretty sure it's not pinching ashtrays from waterside cafés."

They rounded the point and came within sight of the lights of the Hotel Adriatic. A little further and they could see each other's faces. Dora saw his and read there much to disquiet her.

"You're not going to start detecting, Reg!"

"Can't help it, it's in my bones. But I won't let it interfere with your holiday, that's a promise."

———◆———

On Tuesday morning Racic's taxi boat was waiting at the landing stage outside the hotel.

"Gospoda Wexford, it is a great pleasure to meet you."

Courteously he handed Dora into the boat. Its awning of green canvas, now furled, gave it somewhat the look of a gondola. As the engines started, Dora made her excuses for the following day.

"You will like Cetinje," said Racic. "Have a good time. Gospodin Wexford and I will have a bachelor day out. All boys together, eh? Are you quite comfortable? A little more suitable than that one for a lady, I hope."

He pointed across the bay to where a man was paddling a yellow and blue inflatable dinghy. The girl with him wore a very brief bikini. The Nymans.

"If you could manage to avoid passing those people,

Mr. Racic," said Dora, "that would make me very comfortable indeed."

Racic glanced at Wexford. "You have met them? They have annoyed you?"

"Not that. They spoke to us last night in Mirna and the man was rather pushing."

"I will keep close to the shore and cross to Vrt from the small peninsula there."

For most of the morning there was no one else on the little shingly beach of Vrt, which Racic had told them meant a garden. The huddle of cottages behind were overhung with the blue trumpet flowers of the morning glory, and among the walls rose the slender spires of cypress trees. Wexford sat in the shade reading while Dora sunbathed. The dinghy came close only once, but the Wexfords went unrecognised, perhaps because they were in swimming costumes. Iris Nyman stood up briefly before jumping with an explosive splash into the deep water.

"Rude she may be," said Dora, "but I'll grant she's got a lovely figure. And you were wrong about her legs, Reg. Her legs are perfect."

"Didn't notice," said Wexford.

Josip took them back. He was a thin smiling brown man, not unlike Racic, but he had no English beyond "thank you" and "good-bye." They hired him again in the afternoon to take them into Mirna, and they spent a quiet, pleasant evening drinking coffee with Werner and Trudi Muller on the Germans' balcony.

Wednesday came in with a storm at sunrise, and Wexford, watching the lightning and the choppy sea, wondered if Burden had been over-optimistic with his guarantee of fine weather. But by nine the sun was out and the sky clear. He saw Dora off in the Mullers' Mercedes, then walked down to the landing stage. Racic's boat glided in.

"I have brought bread and sausage for our lunch, and Posip in a flask to keep it cool."

"Then we must eat it for our elevenses because I'm taking you out to lunch."

This they ate in Dubrovnik after Racic had taken him to the island of Lokrum. Wexford listened with deepening interest to the boatman-professor's stories. How the ease and wealth of the city merchants had led to a literary renascence, how Dubrovnik-built ships had taken part in the Spanish Armada, how an earthquake had devastated the city and almost destroyed the state. They set off again for Lopud, Sipan and Kolocep, returning across the broad calm waters as the sun began to dip towards the sea.

"Does that little island have a name?" Wexford asked.

"It is called Vrapci, which is to say 'sparrows.' There are thousands of sparrows, so they say, and only sparrows, for no one goes there. One cannot land a boat."

"You mean you can't get off a boat because the rocks are too sheer? What about the other side?"

"I will pull in close and you shall see. There is a beach but no one would wish to use it. Wait."

The island was very small, perhaps no more than half a mile in circumference, and totally overgrown with stunted pines. At their roots the grey rock fell sheer to the water from a height of about ten feet. Racic brought the boat about and they came to the Adriatic side of Vrapci. No sparrows were to be seen, no life of any kind. Between ramparts of rock was a small and forbidding beach of shingle over which an overhanging pine cast deep shade. Looking up at the sky and then down at this dark and stony cove, Wexford could see that, no matter what its altitude, the sun would never penetrate to this beach. Where the shingle narrowed, at the apex, was a cleft in the rock just wide enough to allow the passage of a man's body.

"Not very attractive," he said. "Why should people want to come here?"

"They don't, as far as I know. Except perhaps—well, there is a new fashion, Gospodin Wexford, or Mister as I should call you."

"Call me Reg."

Racic inclined his head. "Reg, yes, thank you. I like the name, though I have not previously encountered it. There is a fashion, as I mentioned, for nude bathing. Here in Yugoslavia we do not allow it, for it is not proper, not decorous. No doubt you have seen painted on some of the rocks the words—in, I fear, lamentable English—'No Nudists.' But there are some who would defy this rule, especially on the small islands. Vrapci might take their fancy if they could find a boat and a boatman to bring them."

"A boat could land on the beach and its occupants swim off the rocks on the other side in the sun."

"If they were good swimmers. But we will not try it, Reg, not at our age being inclined to strip ourselves naked and risk our necks, eh?"

Once more they were off across the wide sea. Wexford looked back to the city walls, those man-made defensive cliffs, and brought himself hesitantly to ask:

"Would you tell me what you overheard of the conversation between that English couple, Philip and Iris Nyman, when you took them out in your boat?"

"So that is their name? Nyman?" He was stalling.

"I have a good reason for asking."

"May I know it?"

Wexford sighed. "I'm a policeman."

Racic's face went very still and tight. "I don't much like that. You were sent here to watch these people? You should have told me before."

"No, Ivo, no." Wexford brought out the unfamiliar name a little self-consciously. "No, you've got me wrong. I never saw or heard of them till last Saturday. But now I've seen them and spoken to them I believe they're doing something illegal. If that's so it's my duty to do something about it. They're my countrymen."

"Reg," said Racic more gently, "what I overheard can have nothing to do with this matter of an illegality. It was personal and private."

"You won't tell me?"

"No. We are not old housewives to spend our time in gossip over the garden walls of our *kucice*, eh?"

Wexford grinned. "Then will you *do* something for me? Will you contrive to let these people know—subtly, of course—that you understand the English language?"

"You are sure that what they are doing is against the law?"

"I am sure. It's drugs or some kind of confidence trick."

There was silence, during which Racic seemed to commune with his sea. Then he said quietly, "I trust you, Reg. Yes, I will do this if I can."

"Then go into Mirna. They're very likely having a drink on the waterfront."

Mirko's boat passed them as they came in and Mirko waved, calling, "*Dobro vece!*"

On the jetty stood a queue of tourists, waiting to be ferried back to the Adriatic or to the hotel at Vrt. There were perhaps a dozen people, and Philip and Iris Nyman brought up the end of the line. It worked out better than Wexford could have hoped. The first four got into Josip's boat, bound for Vrt, the next group into Mirko's which, with its capacity of only eight, was inadequate to take the Nymans.

"Hotel Adriatic," said Philip Nyman. Then he recognised Wexford. "Well, well, we meet again. Had a good day?"

Wexford replied that he had been to Dubrovnik. He helped the girl into the boat. She thanked him, seeming less nervous and even gave him a diffident smile. The motor started and they were off, Racic the anonymous taxi-man, the piece of equipment without which the vehicle won't go.

"I saw you out in your dinghy yesterday," said Wexford.

"Did you?" Philip Nyman seemed gratified. "We can't use it tonight, though. It's not safe after dark and you've really got to be in swimming costumes. We're dining at your hotel with another English couple that we met yesterday and we thought we'd have a romantic walk back along the path."

They were rather more dressed up than usual. Nyman wore a cream-coloured safari suit, his wife a yellow and black dress and high-heeled black sandals. Wexford was on the alert for an invitation to join them for dinner and was surprised when none came.

Both the Nymans lit cigarettes. Wexford noticed Racic stiffen. He had learned enough about the man's principles and shibboleths to be aware of his feelings on pollution. Those cigarette butts would certainly end up in the sea. Anger with his passengers might make him all the more willing to fulfil his promise. But for the moment he remained silent. They rounded the point onto a sea where the sun seemed to have laid a skin of gold.

"So beautiful!" said Iris Nyman.

"A pity you have to go so soon."

"We're staying till Saturday," said Nyman, though without renewing his suggestion that they and the Wexfords should meet again. The girl took a last draw on her cigarette and threw it overboard.

"Oh, well," said Nyman, "there's so much muck in there already, a bit more won't do any harm," and he cast his still-lighted butt into the ripples of melted gold.

They were approaching the hotel landing stage and Racic cut the motor. Nyman felt in his pocket for change. It was Wexford who got up first. He said to Racic as the Yugoslav made the boat fast:

"I've had a splendid day. Thanks very much indeed."

He wasn't looking at them but he fancied the amused glance Nyman would have given his wife at this display of the Englishman's well-known assumption that all but cretins speak his language. Racic drew himself up to his not very great height. What accent he had, what stiltedness and syntactical awkwardness, seemed to be lost. He spoke as if he had been born in Kensington and educated at Oxford.

"I'm glad you enjoyed it, I certainly did. Give my regards to your wife and tell her I hope to see her soon."

There was no sound from the Nymans. They got out of the boat, Racic saying, "Let me give you a hand, madame." Nyman's voice sounded stifled when he produced his twenty dinars and muttered his thanks. Neither said a word to Wexford. They didn't look back. They walked away and his eyes followed them.

"Did I do all right, Reg? I was moved by the foul contamination of my sea."

Absently, still staring, Wexford said, "You did fine."

"What do you look at with such concentration?"

"Legs," said Wexford. "Thanks again. I'll see you tomorrow."

He walked up towards the hotel, looking for them, but they were nowhere in sight. On the terrace he turned and looked back and there they were, walking hurriedly along the waterfront path back to Mirna, their new friends and their dinner engagement forgotten. Wexford went into the hotel and took the lift up to his room. Dora wasn't back yet. Feeling rather shaken, he lay down on one of the twin beds. This latest development or discovery was, at any rate, far from what he had expected. And what now? Somehow get hold of the Dubrovnik police? He reached for the phone to call reception but dropped it again when Dora walked in.

She came up to him in consternation. "Are you all right, darling?"

His blood pressure, his heart, too much sun—he could tell what she was thinking. It was rare for him to take a rest in the daytime. "Of course I am. I'm fine." He sat up. "Dora, something most peculiar . . ."

"You're detecting again! I knew it." She kicked off her shoes and threw open the doors to the balcony. "You haven't even asked me if I've had a nice day."

"I can see you have. Come in, my dear, don't be difficult. I always like to think you're the only woman I know who isn't difficult." She looked at him warily. "Listen," he said. "Do something for me. Describe the woman we saw on the walls."

"Iris Nyman? What do you mean?"

"Just do as I ask, there's a good girl."

"You're mad. You *have* had a touch of the sun. Well, I suppose if it humours you. . . . Medium height, good figure, very tanned, about thirty, geometric haircut. She was wearing a jade green halter top and a blue and green and pink skirt."

"Now describe the woman we saw with Nyman on Monday."

"There's no difference except for a black top and a stole."

Wexford nodded. He got off the bed, walked past her on to the balcony and said:

"They're not the same woman."

———◄◆►———

"What on earth are you suggesting?"

"I wish I knew," said Wexford, "but I do know the Iris Nyman we saw on the walls is not the Iris Nyman I saw in Mirna on Monday morning and we saw that night and we saw yesterday and I saw this evening."

"You're letting your imagination run away with you. You are, Reg. That hair, for instance, it was striking, and those clothes, and being with Philip Nyman."

"Don't you see you've named the very things that would be used to make anyone think they're the same woman? Neither of us saw her face that first time. Neither of us heard her voice. We only noticed the striking things about her."

"What makes you think they're not the same?"

"Her legs. The legs are different. You drew my attention to them. One might say you set me off on this."

Dora leaned over the balcony rail. Her shoulders sagged. "Then I wish I hadn't. Reg, you never discuss cases with me at home. Why do it here?"

"There's no one else."

"Thanks very much. All this about her not being the same woman, it's nonsense, you've dreamed it up. Why would anyone try and fake a thing like that? Come to that, *how* could anyone?"

"Easily. All you need is a female accomplice of similar

build and age. On Saturday or Sunday this accomplice had her hair cut and dyed and assumed Iris Nyman's clothes. I mean to find out why."

Dora turned her back on the sunset and fixed him with a cold and stony look. "No, Reg, no. I'm not being difficult. I'm just behaving like any normal woman would when she goes on holiday and finds her husband can't leave his job at home for just two weeks. This is the first foreign holiday I've had in ten years. If you'd been sent here to watch these people, if it was work, I wouldn't say a word. But it's just something you've dreamed up because you can't relax and enjoy the sun and the sea like other people."

"OK," said her husband, "look at it that way." He was very fond of his wife, he valued her and quickly felt guilt over his frequent enforced neglect of her. This time any neglect would be as if by design, the result of that bone-deep need of his to unravel mysteries. "Don't give me that Gorgon face. I've said I won't let this spoil your holiday and I won't." He touched her cheek, gently rubbing it. "And now I'm going to have my bath."

Not much more than twelve hours later he was walking the path to Mirna. The sun was already hot and there was a speedboat out in the bay. Carpet sellers had spread their wares in the market place, and the cafés were open for those who wanted coffee or—even at this hour—plum brandy.

The Bosnia, most of it mercifully concealed by pines and ranks of cypresses, looked from close to, with its floors in plate-like layers and its concrete flying buttresses, more like an Unidentified Flying Object come to rest in the woods than a holiday hotel. Wexford crossed a forecourt as big as a football pitch and entered a foyer that wouldn't have disgraced some capital city's palace of justice.

The receptionist spoke good English.

"Mr. and Mrs. Nyman checked out last evening, sir."

"Surely they expected to stay another three days?"

"I cannot tell you, sir. They left last evening before dinner. I cannot help you more."

So that was that.

"What are you going to do now?" said Dora over a late breakfast. "Have a hilarious cops and robbers car chase up the Dalmatian coast?"

"I'm going to wait and see. And in the meantime I'm going to enjoy my holiday and see that you enjoy yours." He watched her relax and smile for the first time since the previous evening.

The Nymans were at the back of his mind all the time, but he did manage to enjoy the rest of his holiday. Werner and Trudi took them to Mostar to see the Turkish bridge. They went on a coach to Budva, and the members of the taxi boat syndicate ferried them from Mirna to Vrt and out to Lokrum. It was in secret that Wexford daily bought a London newspaper, a day old and three times its normal price. He wasn't sure why he did so, what he hoped or feared. On their last morning he nearly didn't bother. After all, he would be home in not much more than twenty-four hours and then he would have to take some action. But as he passed the reception desk, Dora having already entered the dining room for breakfast, the clerk held out the newspaper to him as a matter of course.

Wexford thanked him—and there it was on the front page.

Disappearance of Tycoon's Daughter, said the headline. *Beachwear King Fears Kidnap Plot.*

The text beneath read: "Mrs. Iris Nyman, 32, failed to return to her North London home from a shopping expedition yesterday. Her father, Mr. James Woodhouse, Chairman of Sunsports Ltd., a leading manufacturer of beachwear, fears his daughter may have been kidnapped and expects a ransom demand. Police are taking a serious view.

"Mrs. Nyman's husband, 33-year-old Philip Nyman, said at the couple's home in Flask Walk, Hampstead, today, 'My wife and I had just got back from a motoring holiday in Italy and Yugoslavia. On the following morning Iris went out shopping and never returned. I am frantic with worry. She seemed to be happy and relaxed.'

"Mr. Woodhouse's company of which Mrs. Nyman is a director was this year involved in a vast takeover bid as a result of which two other major clothing firms were absorbed into Sunsports Ltd. The company's turnover last year was in the region of £100,000,000."

There was a photograph of Iris Nyman in black glasses. Wexford would have been hard put to it to say whether this was of the woman on the walls or the woman in Mirna.

That night they gave Racic a farewell dinner at the Dubrovacka restaurant.

"Don't say what they all say, Reg, that you will come back next year. Dalmatia is beautiful to you and Gospoda Wexford now, but a few days and the memory will fade. Someone will say, San Marino for you next time, or Ibiza, and there you will go. Is it not so?"

"I said I shall be back," said Wexford, "and I meant it." He raised his glass of Posip. "But not in a year's time. It'll be sooner than that."

Three hundred and sixty-two days sooner, as Racic pointed out.

"And here I am, sitting in the *vrt* of your *kucica!*"

"Reg, we shall have you fluent in Serbo-Croat yet."

"Alas, no. I must be back in London again tomorrow night."

They were in Racic's garden, halfway up the terraced hill behind Mirna, sitting in wicker chairs under his vine and his fig tree. Pink and white and red oleanders shimmered in the dusk, and above their heads bunches of small green grapes hung between the slats of a canopy. On the table was a bottle of Posip and the remains of a dinner of king prawns and Dalmatian buttered potatoes, salad and bread and big ripe peaches.

"And now we have eaten," said Racic, "you will please tell me the tale of the important business that brought you back to Mirna so pleasantly soon. It concerns Mr. and Mrs. Nyman?"

"Ivo, we shall have you a policeman yet."

Racic laughed and re-filled Wexford's glass. Then he looked serious. "Not a laughing matter, I think, not pleasant."

"Far from it. Iris Nyman is dead, murdered, unless I am much mistaken. This afternoon I accompanied the Dubrovnik police out into the bay and we took her body out of the cave on Vrapci."

"*Zaboga!* You cannot mean it! That girl who was at the Bosnia and who came out with her husband in my boat?"

"Well, no, not that one. She's alive and in Athens from where, I imagine, she'll be extradited."

"I don't understand. Tell me the tale from the beginning."

Wexford leaned back in his chair and looked up through the vines at the violet sky where the first stars had begun to show. "I'll have to start with the background," he said, and after a pause, "Iris Nyman was the daughter and only child of James Woodhouse, the chairman of a company called Sunsports Ltd. which makes sports- and beachwear and has a large export trade. She married when she was very young, less than twenty, a junior salesman in her father's firm. After the marriage Woodhouse made a director of her, settled a lot of money on her, bought her a house and gave her a company car. To justify her company fees and expenses, she was in the habit of annually making a trip to holiday resorts in Europe with her husband, ostensibly to wear Sunsports clothes and note who else was wearing them, and also to study the success of rival markets. Probably, she simply holidayed.

"The marriage was not a happy one. At any rate, Philip Nyman wasn't happy. Iris was a typically arrogant rich girl who expected always to have her own way. Besides, the money and the house and the car were all hers. He remained a salesman. Then, a year or so ago, he fell in love with a cousin of Iris's, a girl called Anna Ashby. Apparently, Iris knew nothing about this, and her father certainly didn't."

"Then how can you . . . ?" Racic interrupted.

"These affairs are always known to someone, Ivo. One of Anna's friends has made a statement to Scotland Yard." Wexford paused and drank some of his wine. "That's the background," he said. "Now for what happened a month or so ago.

"The Nymans had arranged to motor down as usual to the South of France, but this time to cross northern Italy and spend a week or ten days here on the Dalmatian coast. Anna Ashby had planned to spend part of the summer with friends in Greece so, *at Iris's invitation*, she was to accompany the Nymans as far as Dubrovnik where she would stay a few days with them, then go on by air to Athens.

"In Dubrovnik, after the three of them had been there a few days, Iris got hold of the idea of bathing off Vrapci. Perhaps she wanted to bathe in the nude, perhaps she had already been on the "topless" beach at St. Tropez. I don't know. Philip Nyman has admitted nothing of this. Up until the time I left, he was still insisting that his wife had returned to England with him."

"It was your idea, then," put in Racic, "that this poor woman's body was concealed on the isle of sparrows?"

"It was a guess," said Wexford. "I overheard some words, I was later told a lie. I'm a policeman. Whether they went to Vrapci on Saturday, June 18th, or Sunday, June 19th, I can't tell you. Suffice that they did go—in that inflatable dinghy of theirs. The three of them went but only two came back, Nyman and Anna Ashby."

"They killed Mrs. Nyman?"

Wexford looked thoughtful. "I think so, certainly. Of course there's a possibility that she drowned, that it was an accident. But in that case wouldn't any normal husband have immediately informed the proper authority? If he had recovered the body, wouldn't he have brought it back with him? We're awaiting the results of the post-mortem, but even if that shows no wounds or bruises on the body, even if the lungs are full of water, I should be very surprised to learn that Nyman and, or, Anna hadn't hastened her death or watched her drown."

Both were silent for a moment, Racic nodding slowly as he digested what Wexford had told him. Then he got up and fetched from the house a candelabrum, but thinking better of it, switched on an electric lamp attached to the wall.

"Any light will attract the insects, but there at least they will not trouble us. So it was this Anna Ashby who came to Mirna, posing as Mrs. Nyman?"

"According to the manager of the hotel in Dubrovnik where the three of them had been staying, Nyman checked out and paid his bill early on the evening of the 19th. Neither of the women was with him. Iris was dead and Anna was at the hairdresser's, having her hair cut and dyed to the same style and colour as her cousin's. The police have already found the hairdresser who did the job."

"They came here next," said Racic. "Why didn't they go straight back to England? And now I must ask, surely they did not intend to play this game in England? Even if the two women, as cousins, to a degree resembled each other, this Anna could not hope to deceive a father, close friends, Mrs. Nyman's neighbours."

"The answer to your first question is that to have returned to England a week earlier than expected would have looked odd. Why go back? The weather was perfect. Nyman wanted to give the impression they had both been well and happy during their holiday. No, his idea was to make sufficient people here in Yugoslavia believe that Iris was alive after June 19th. That's why he latched on to us and got our name and home town out of us. He wanted to be sure of witnesses if need be. Anna was less bold, she was frightened to death. But Philip actually found himself two more English witnesses, though, thanks to your intervention, he never kept the appointment to dine with them."

"My intervention?"

"Your excellent English. And now perhaps you'll tell me what you overheard in the boat."

Racic laughed. His strong white teeth gleamed in the

lamplight. "I knew she was not Mrs. Nyman, Reg, but that knowledge would not have helped you then, eh? You had seen the lady on the walls but not, I presume, her marriage document. I thought to myself, why should I tell this busybody of a policeman the secrets of my passengers? But now, to use an idiom, here goes. Reg, the lady said, 'I feel so guilty, it is terrible what we have done,' and he replied, 'Everyone here thinks you are my wife, and no one at home will suspect a thing. One day you will be and we shall forget all this.' Now, would you have supposed they were talking of murder or of illicit passion?"

Wexford smiled. "Nyman must have thought we'd confer, you and I, and jump to the former conclusion. Or else he'd forgotten what he'd said. He has rather a way of doing that."

"And after they left?"

"Anna was to travel on Iris's passport in the hope it would be stamped at at least one frontier. In fact, it was stamped at two, between Yugoslavia and Italy and again at Calais. At Dover Anna presumably left him and caught the first plane to Athens she could get. Nyman went home, reaching there in the night of the 28th, the precise date on which he and Iris had planned to return. On the following afternoon he told his father-in-law and the police that Iris was missing."

"He hoped the search for her or her body," said Racic, "would be confined to England because he had incontrovertible proof she had stayed with him in Mirna and had travelled back with him to England. No one would think of looking for her here, for it was known to many witnesses that she left here alive. But what did he hope to gain? Surely, if your laws are like ours, and I believe all laws are alike in this, without her body it would be years before he could inherit her money or marry again?"

"You have to remember this wasn't a premeditated murder. It must have happened on the spur of the moment. So conceal the body where it may never be found or not found until it's beyond identification, announce that his wife has gone missing in England, and he gets the sympathy of his powerful father-in-law and certainly Iris's house to live in and Iris's car to drive. He keeps his job which he would have lost had he divorced Iris, and very likely gets all or some of her allowance transferred to him. Anna gets her hair back to its natural colour—brown, incidentally—lets it grow out, returns home and they resume their friendship. One day Iris will be presumed dead and they can marry."

Racic cut himself a slice of bread and nibbled at an olive. "I see it all or nearly all. I see that, but for your presence here in Mirna, the conspiracy had every chance of success. What I don't see is, if this woman made herself look so much like this woman you saw on the walls, if she had the same hair and clothes—but I am a fool! You saw her face."

"I didn't see her face and I didn't hear her voice. Dora and I saw her very briefly and then only from the back."

"It is beyond my comprehension."

"The legs," said Wexford. "The legs were different."

"But, my dear Reg, my dear policeman, surely the leg of one brown-skinned slender young woman is much like the leg of such another? Or was there a mole perhaps or a protruding vein?"

"Not as far as I know. The only time I saw the true Iris Nyman she wore a skirt that covered her legs to mid-calf. In fact, I could see very little of her legs."

"Then I am flummoxed."

"Ankles," said Wexford. "There are two types of normal ankle in this world, and the difference between them can only be seen from the back. In one type the calf seems to join the heel with a narrowing but no distinct shaft. In the other, the type of beauty, the Achilles tendon makes a long slender shaft with deep indentations on either side of it beneath the ankle bones. I saw Iris Nyman's legs only from behind and in her the Achilles tendon was not apparent. It was a flaw in her appearance. When I first noticed Anna Ashby's legs from behind as she was getting off your boat, I observed the long shaft of the tendon leading up into the muscle of a shapely calf. She had no flaw in her legs, but you might call that perfection her Achilles Heel."

"*Zaboga!* Beauty, eh? Only two types in the world?" Racic extended one foot and rolled up his trouser leg. Wexford's was already rucked up. In the lamplight they peered down at each other's calves from behind. "Yours are all right," said Racic. "In fact, they are fine. In the beauty class."

"So are yours, you old professor and boatman."

Racic burst out laughing. "*Tesko meni!* Two elderly gentlemen who should know better, airing their limbs in an ankle competition! Whatever next?"

"Well, I shouldn't," said Wexford, "but next let's finish up the Posip."

When the Wedding Was Over

"Matrimony," said Chief Inspector Wexford, "begins with dearly beloved and ends with amazement."

His wife, sitting beside him on the bridegroom's side of the church, whispered, "What did you say?"

He repeated it. She steadied the large floral hat which her husband had called becoming but not exactly conducive to *sotto voce* intimacies. "What on earth makes you say that?"

"Thomas Hardy. He said it first. But look in your Prayer Book."

The bridegroom waited, hang-dog, with his best man. Michael Burden was very much in love, was entering this second marriage with someone admirably suited to him, had agreed with his fiancée that nothing but a religious ceremony would do for them, yet at forty-four was a little superannuated for what Wexford called "all this white wedding gubbins." There were two hundred people in the church. Burden, his best man and his ushers were in morning dress. Madonna lilies and stephanotis and syringa decorated the pews, the pulpit and the chancel steps. It was the kind of thing that is properly designed for someone twenty years younger. Burden had been through it before when he *was* twenty years younger. Wexford chuckled silently, looking at the anxious face above the high white collar. And then as Dora, leafing through the marriage service, said, "Oh, I *see*," the organist went from voluntaries into the opening bars of the Lohengrin march and Jenny Ireland appeared at the church door on her father's arm.

A beautiful bride, of course. Seven years younger than Burden, blonde, gentle, low-voiced, and given to radiant smiles. Jenny's father gave her hand into Burden's and the Rector of St. Peter's began:

"Dearly beloved, we are gathered together . . ."

While bride and groom were being informed that marriage was not for the satisfaction of their carnal lusts, and that they must bring up their children in a Christian manner, Wexford studied the congregation. In front of himself and Dora sat Burden's sister-in-law, Grace, whom everyone had thought he would marry after the death of his first wife. But Burden had found consolation with a redheaded woman, wild and sweet and strange, gone now God knew where, and Grace had married someone else. Two little boys now sat between Grace and that someone else, giving their parents a full-time job keeping them quiet.

Burden's mother and father were both dead. Wexford thought he recognised, from one meeting a dozen years before, an aged aunt. Beside her sat Dr. Crocker and his wife, beyond them and behind were a crowd whose individual members he knew either only by sight or not at all. Sylvia, his elder daughter, was sitting on his other side, his grandsons between her and their father, and at the central aisle end of the pew, Sheila Wexford of the Royal Shakespeare Company. Wexford's actress daughter, who on her entry had commanded nudges, whispers, every gaze, sat looking with unaccustomed wistfulness at Jenny Ireland in her clouds of white and wreath of pearls.

"I, Michael George, take thee, Janina, to my wedded wife, to have and to hold from this day forward . . ."

Janina. *Janina?* Wexford had supposed her name was Jennifer. What sort of parents called a daughter Janina? Turks? Fans of Dumas? He leaned forward to get a good look at these philonomatous progenitors. They looked ordinary enough, Mr. Ireland apparently exhausted by the effort of giving the bride away, Jenny's mother making use of the lace handkerchief provided for the specific purpose of crying into it those tears of joy and loss. What romantic streak had led them to dismiss Elizabeth and Susan and Anne in favour of—Janina?

"Those whom God hath joined together, let no man put asunder. Forasmuch as Michael George and Janina have consented together in holy wedlock . . ."

Had they been as adventurous in the naming of their son? All Wexford could see of him was a broad back, a bit of profile, and now a hand. The hand was passing a large white handkerchief to his mother. Wexford found himself being suddenly yanked to his feet to sing a hymn.

"O Perfect Love, all human thought transcending,
Lowly we kneel in prayer before Thy throne . . ."

These words had the effect of evoking from Mrs. Ireland audible sobs. Her son—hadn't Burden said he was in publishing?—looked embarrassed, turning his head. A young woman, strangely dressed in black with an orange hat, edged past the publisher to put a consoling arm round his mother.

"O Lord, save Thy servant and Thy handmaid."

"Who put their trust in Thee," said Dora and most of the rest of the congregation.

"O Lord, send them help from Thy holy place."

Wexford, to show team spirit, said, "Amen," and when

everyone else said, "And evermore defend them," decided to keep quiet in future.

Mrs. Ireland had stopped crying. Wexford's gaze drifted to his own daughters, Sheila singing lustily, Sylvia, the Women's Liberationist, with less assurance as if she doubted the ethics of lending her support to so archaic and sexist a ceremony. His grandsons were beginning to fidget.

"Almighty God, who at the beginning did create our first parents, Adam and Eve . . ."

Dear Mike, thought Wexford with a flash of sentimentality that came to him perhaps once every ten years, you'll be OK now. No more carnal lusts conflicting with a puritan conscience, no more loneliness, no more worrying about those selfish kids of yours, no more temptation-of-St.-Anthony stuff. For is it not ordained as a remedy against sin, and to avoid fornication, that such persons as have not the gift of continency may marry and keep themselves undefiled?

"For after this manner in the old time the holy women who trusted in God . . ."

He was quite surprised that they were using the ancient form. Still, the bride had promised to obey. He couldn't resist glancing at Sylvia.

". . . being in subjection to their own husbands . . ."

Her face was a study in incredulous dismay as she mouthed at her sister "Unbelievable" and "antique."

". . . Even as Sarah obeyed Abraham, calling him Lord, whose daughters ye are as long as ye do well, and are not afraid with any amazement."

At the Olive and Dove hotel there was a reception line to greet guests, Mrs. Ireland smiling, re-rouged and restored, Burden looking like someone who has had an operation and been told the prognosis is excellent, Jenny serene as a bride should be.

Dry sherry and white wine on trays. No champagne. Wexford remembered that there was a younger Ireland daughter, absent with her husband in some dreadful place—Botswana? Lesotho? No doubt all the champagne funds had been expended on her. It was a buffet lunch, but a good one. Smoked salmon and duck and strawberries. Nobody, he said to himself, has ever really thought of anything better to eat than smoked salmon and duck and strawberries unless it might be caviare and grouse and syllabub. He was weighing the two menus against one another, must without knowing it have been thinking aloud, for a voice said:

, "Asparagus, trout, apple pie."

"Well, maybe," said Wexford, "but I do like meat. Trout's a bit insipid. You're Jenny's brother, I'm sorry I don't remember your name. How d'you do?"

"How d'you do? I know who you are. Mike told me. I'm Amyas Ireland."

So that funny old pair hadn't had a one-off indulgence when they had named Janina. Again Wexford's thoughts seemed revealed to this intuitive person.

"Oh, I know," said Ireland, "but how about my other sister? She's called Cunegonde. Her husband calls her Queenie. Look, I'd like to talk to you. Could we get together a minute away from all this crush? Mike was going to help me out, but I can't ask him now, not when he's off on his honeymoon. It's about a book we're publishing."

The girl in black and orange, Burden's nephews, Sheila Wexford, Burden's best man and a gaggle of children, all carrying plates, passed between them at this point. It was at least a minute before Wexford could ask, "Who's we?"

and another half-minute before Amyas Ireland understood what he meant.

"Carlyon Brent," he said, his mouth full of duck. "I'm
with Carlyon Brent."

One of the largest and most distinguished of publishing
houses. Wexford was impressed. "You published the Vandrian, didn't you, and the de Coverley books?"

Ireland nodded. "Mike said you were a great reader.
That's good. Can I get you some more duck? No? I'm
going to. I won't be a minute." Enviously Wexford
watched him shovel fat-rimmed slices of duck breast on
to his plate, take a brioche, have second thoughts and
take another. The man was as thin as a rail too, posi-
tively emaciated.

"I look after the crime list," he said as he sat down
again. "As I said, Mike half-promised . . . This isn't
fiction, it's fact. The Winchurch case?"

"Ah."

"I know it's a bit of a nerve asking, but would you read
a manuscript for me?"

Wexford took a cup of coffee from a passing tray.
"What for?"

"Well, in the interests of truth. Mike was going to tell
me what he thought." Wexford looked at him dubiously.
He had the highest respect and the deepest affection for
Inspector Burden but he was one of the last people he
would have considered as a literary critic. "To tell me
what he thought," the publisher said once again. "You
see, it's worrying me. The author has discovered some
new facts and they more or less prove Mrs. Winchurch's
innocence." He hesitated. "Have you ever heard of a
writer called Kenneth Gandolph?"

Wexford was saved from answering by the pounding of
a gavel on the top table and the beginning of the

speeches. A great many toasts had been drunk, several dozen telegrams read out, and the bride and groom departed to change their clothes before he had an opportunity to reply to Ireland's question. And he was glad of the respite, for what he knew of Gandolph, though based on hearsay, was not prepossessing.

"Doesn't he write crime novels?" he said when the enquiry was repeated. "And the occasional examination of a real-life crime?"

Nodding, Ireland said, "It's good, this script of his. We want to do it for next spring's list. It's an eighty-year-old murder, sure, but people are still fascinated by it. I think this new version could cause quite a sensation."

"Florence Winchurch was hanged," said Wexford, "yet there was always some margin of doubt about her guilt. Where does Gandolph get his fresh facts from?"

"May I send you a copy of the script? You'll find all that in the introduction."

Wexford shrugged, then smiled. "I suppose so. You do realise I can't do more than maybe spot mistakes in forensics? I did say maybe, mind." But his interest had already been caught. It made him say, "Florence was married at St. Peter's, you know, and she also had her wedding reception here."

"And spent part of her honeymoon in Greece."

"No doubt the parallels end there," said Wexford as Burden and Jenny came back into the room.

Burden was in a grey lounge suit, she in pale blue sprigged muslin. Wexford felt an absurd impulse of tenderness towards him. It was partly caused by Jenny's hat which she would never wear again, would never have occasion to wear, would remove the minute they got into the car. But Burden was the sort of man who could never be happy with a woman who didn't have a hat as part of her "going-away" costume. His own clothes were eminently unsuitable for flying to Crete in June. They both looked very happy and embarrassed.

Mrs. Ireland seized her daughter in a crushing embrace.

"It's not for ever, Mother," said Jenny. "It's only for two weeks."

"Well, in a way," said Burden. He shook hands gravely with his own son, down from university for the weekend, and planted a kiss on his daughter's forehead. Must have been reading novels, Wexford thought, grinning to himself.

"Good luck, Mike," he said.

The bride took his hand, put a soft cool kiss on to the corner of his mouth. Say I'm growing old but add, Jenny kissed me. He didn't say that aloud. He nodded and smiled and took his wife's arm and frowned at Sylvia's naughty boys like the patriarch he was. Burden and Jenny went out to the car which had Just Married written in lipstick on the rear window and a shoe tied on the back bumper.

There was a clicking of handbag clasps, a flurry of hands, and then a tempest of confetti broke over them.

It was an isolated house, standing some twenty yards back from the Myringham road. Plumb in the centre of the façade was a plaque bearing the date 1896. Wexford had often thought that there seemed to have been positive intent on the part of late-Victorian builders to design and erect houses that were not only ugly, complex and inconvenient, but also distinctly sinister in appearance. The Limes, though well-maintained and set in a garden as multi-coloured, cushiony and floral as a quilt, nevertheless kept this sinister quality. Khaki-coloured brick and grey slate had been the principal materials used in its construction. Without being able to define exactly how, Wexford could see that, in relation to the walls, the proportions of the sash windows were wrong. A turret grew out of each of the front corners and each of these turrets was topped by a conical roof, giving the place the look of a cross between Balmoral castle and a hotel in Kitzbuehl. The lime trees which gave it its name had been lopped so many times since their planting at the turn of the century that now they were squat and misshapen.

In the days of the Winchurches it had been called Paraleash House. But this name, of historical significance on account of its connection with the ancient manor of Paraleash, had been changed specifically as a result of the murder of Edward Winchurch. Even so, it had stood empty for ten years. Then it had found a buyer a year or so before the First World War, a man who was killed in that war. Its present owner had occupied it for half a dozen years, and in the time intervening between his purchase of it and 1918 it had been variously a nursing home, the annexe of an agricultural college and a private school. The owner was a retired brigadier. As he emerged from the front door with two sealyhams on a lead, Wexford retreated to his car and drove home.

It was Monday evening and Burden's marriage was two days old. Monday was the evening of Dora's pottery class, the fruits of which, bruised-looking and not invariably symmetrical, were scattered haphazardly about the room like windfalls. Hunting along the shelves for G. Hallam Saul's *When the Summer Is Shed* and *The Trial of Florence Winchurch* from the Notable British Trials series, he nearly knocked over one of those rotund yet lopsided objects. With a sigh of relief that it was unharmed, he set about refreshing his memory of the Winchurch case with the help of Miss Saul's classic.

———————◄◆►———————

Florence May Anstruther had been nineteen at the time of her marriage to Edward Winchurch and he forty-seven. She was a good-looking fair-haired girl, rather tall and Junoesque, the daughter of a Kingsmarkham chemist —that is, a pharmacist, for her father had kept a shop in the High Street. In 1895 this damned her as of no account in the social hierarchy, and few people would have bet much on her chances of marrying well. But she did. Winchurch was a barrister who, at this stage of his life, practised law from inclination rather than from need. His father, a Sussex landowner, had died some three years before and had left him what for the last decade of the nineteenth century was an enormous fortune, two hundred thousand pounds. Presumably, he had been attracted to Florence by her youth, her looks and her lady-like ways. She had been given the best education, including six months at a finishing school, that the chemist could afford. Winchurch's attraction for Florence was generally supposed to have been solely his money.

They were married in June 1895 at the parish church of St. Peter's, Kingsmarkham, and went on a six-months honeymoon, touring Italy, Greece, and the Swiss Alps. When they returned home Winchurch took a lease of Sewingbury Priory while building began on Paraleash House, and it may have been that the conical roofs on those turrets were inspired directly by what Florence had seen on her alpine travels. They moved into the lavishly furnished new house in May 1896, and Florence settled down to the life of a Victorian lady with a wealthy husband and a staff of indoor and outdoor servants. A vapid life at best, even if alleviated by a brood of children. But Florence had no children and was to have none.

Once or twice a week Edward Winchurch went up to London by the train from Kingsmarkham, as commuters had done before and have been doing ever since. Florence gave orders to her cook, arranged the flowers, paid and received calls, read novels and devoted a good many hours a day to her face, her hair and her dress. Local opinion of the couple at that time seemed to have been that they were as happy as most people, that Florence had done very well for herself and knew it, and Edward not so badly as had been predicted.

In the autumn of 1896 a young doctor of medicine bought a practice in Kingsmarkham and came to live there with his unmarried sister. Their name was Fenton. Frank Fenton was an extremely handsome man, twenty-six years old, six feet tall, with jet black hair, a Byronic eye and an arrogant lift to his chin. The sister was called Ada, and she was neither good-looking nor arrogant, being partly crippled by poliomyelitis which had left her with one leg badly twisted and paralysed.

It was ostensibly to befriend Ada Fenton that Florence first began calling at the Fentons' house in Queen Street. Florence professed great affection for Ada, took her about in her carriage and offered her the use of it whenever she had to go any distance. From this it was an obvious step to persuade Edward that Frank Fenton should become the Winchurches' doctor. Within another few months young Mrs. Winchurch had become the doctor's mistress.

It was probable that Ada knew nothing, or next to nothing, about it. In the eighteen-nineties a young girl could be, and usually was, very innocent. At the trial it was stated by Florence's coachman that he would be sent to the Fentons' house several times a week to take Miss

Fenton driving, while Ada's housemaid said that Mrs. Winchurch would arrive on foot soon after Miss Fenton had gone out and be admitted rapidly through a french window by the doctor himself. During the winter of 1898 it seemed likely that Frank Fenton had performed an abortion on Mrs. Winchurch, and for some months afterwards they met only at social gatherings and occasionally when Florence was visiting Ada. But their feelings for each other were too strong for them to bear separation and by the following summer they were again meeting at Fenton's house while Ada was out, and now also at Paraleash House on the days when Edward had departed for the law courts.

Divorce was difficult but by no means impossible or unheard-of in 1899. At the trial Frank Fenton said he had wanted Mrs. Winchurch to ask her husband for a divorce. He would have married her in spite of the disastrous effect on his career. It was she, he said, who refused to consider it on the grounds that she did not think she could bear the disgrace.

In January 1900 Florence went to London for the day and, among other purchases, bought at a grocer's two cans of herring fillets marinaded in a white wine sauce. It was rare for canned food to appear in the Winchurch household, and when Florence suggested that these herring fillets should be used in the preparation of a dish called *Filets de hareng marinés à la Rosette,* the recipe for which she had been given by Ada Fenton, the cook, Mrs. Eliza Holmes, protested that she could prepare it from fresh fish. Florence, however, insisted, one of the cans was used, and the dish was made and served to Florence and Edward at dinner. It was brought in by the parlourmaid, Alice Evans, as a savoury or final course to a four-course meal. Although Florence had shown so much enthusiasm about the dish, she took none of it. Edward ate a moderate amount and the rest was removed to the kitchen where it was shared between Mrs. Holmes, Alice Evans and the housemaid, Violet Stedman. No one suffered any ill-effects. The date was 30 January 1900.

Five weeks later on 5 March Florence asked Mrs. Holmes to make the dish again, using the remaining can, as her husband had liked it so much. This time Florence too partook of the marinaded herrings, but when the remains of it were about to be removed by Alice to the kitchen, she advised her to tell the others not to eat it as she "thought it had a strange taste and was perhaps not quite fresh." However, although Mrs. Holmes and Alice abstained, Violet Stedman ate a larger quantity of the dish than had either Florence or Edward.

Florence, as was her habit, left Edward to drink his port alone. Within a few minutes a strangled shout was heard from the dining room and a sound as of furniture breaking. Florence and Alice Evans and Mrs. Holmes went into the room and found Edward Winchurch lying on the floor, a chair with one leg wrenched from its socket tipped over beside him and an overturned glass of port on the table. Florence approached him and he went into a violent convulsion, arching his back and baring his teeth, his hands grasping the chair in apparent agony.

John Barstow, the coachman, was sent to fetch Dr. Fenton. By this time Florence was complaining of stomach pains and seemed unable to stand. Fenton arrived, had Edward and Florence removed upstairs and asked Mrs. Holmes what they had eaten. She showed him the empty herring fillets can, and he recognised the brand as that by which a patient of a colleague of his had recently been infected with botulism, a virulent and usually fatal form of food poisoning. Fenton immediately assumed that

it was *bacillus botulinus* which had attacked the Winchurches, and such is the power of suggestion that Violet
Stedman now said she felt sick and faint.

Botulism causes paralysis, difficulty in breathing and a
disturbance of the vision. Florence appeared to be partly
paralysed and said she had double vision. Edward's symptoms were different. He continued to have spasms, was
totally relaxed between spasms, and although he had
difficulty in breathing and other symptoms of botulism,
the onset had been exceptionally rapid for any form of
food poisoning. Fenton, however, had never seen a case
of botulism, which is extremely rare, and he supposed
that the symptoms would vary greatly from person to person. He gave jalap and cream of tartar as a purgative and,
in the absence of any known relatives of Edward Winchurch, he sent for Florence's father, Thomas Anstruther.

If Fenton was less innocent than was supposed, he had
made a mistake in sending for Anstruther, for Florence's
father insisted on a second opinion, and at ten o'clock
went himself to the home of that very colleague of Fenton's who had recently witnessed a known case of botulism. This was Dr. Maurice Waterfield, twice Fenton's
age, a popular man with a large practice in Stowerton. He
looked at Edward Winchurch, at the agonised grin which
overspread his features, and as Edward went into his last
convulsive seizure, pronounced that he had been poi-
soned not by *bacillus botulinus* but by strychnine.

Edward died a few minutes afterwards. Dr. Waterfield
told Fenton that there was nothing physically wrong with
either Florence or Violet Stedman. The former was suffering from shock or "neurasthenia," the latter from indiges-
tion brought on by over-eating. The police were informed, an inquest took place, and after it Florence was
immediately arrested and charged with murdering her

husband by administering to him a noxious substance, to wit *strychnos nux vomica,* in a decanter of port wine.

Her trial took place in London at the Central Criminal Court. She was twenty-four years old, a beautiful woman, and was by then known to have been having a love affair with the young and handsome Dr. Fenton. As such, she and her case attracted national attention. Fenton had by then lost his practice, lost all hope of succeeding with another in the British Isles, and even before the trial his name had become a by-word, scurrilous doggerel being sung about him and Florence in the music halls. But far from increasing his loyalty to Florence, this seemed to make him the more determined to dissociate himself from her. He appeared as the prosecution's principal witness, and it was his evidence which sent Florence to the gallows.

Fenton admitted his relationship with Florence but said that he had told her it must end. The only possible alternative was divorce and ultimately marriage to himself. In early January 1900 Florence had been calling on his sister Ada, and he had come in to find them looking through a book of recipes. One of the recipes called for the use of herring fillets marinaded in white wine sauce, the mention of which had caused him to tell them about a case of botulism which a patient of Dr. Waterfield's was believed to have contracted from eating the contents of a can of just such fillets. He had named the brand and advised his sister not to buy any of that kind. When, some seven weeks later, he was called to the dying Edward Winchurch, the cook had shown him an empty can of that very brand. In his opinion, Mrs. Winchurch herself was not ill at all, was not even ill from "nerves" but was shamming. The judge said that he was not there to give his opinion, but the warning came too late. To the jury the point had already been made.

Asked if he was aware that strychnine had therapeutic uses in small quantities, Fenton said he was but that he kept none in his dispensary. In any case, his dispensary was kept locked and the cupboards inside it locked, so it would have been impossible for Florence to have entered it or to have appropriated anything while on a visit to Ada. Ada Fenton was not called as a witness. She was ill, suffering from what her doctor, Dr. Waterfield, called "brain fever."

The prosecution's case was that, in order to inherit his fortune and marry Dr. Fenton, Florence Winchurch had attempted to poison her husband with infected fish, or fish she had good reason to suppose might be infected. When this failed she saw to it that the dish was provided again, and herself added strychnine to the port decanter. It was postulated that she obtained the strychnine from her father's shop, without his knowledge, where it was kept in stock for the destruction of rats and moles. After her husband was taken ill, she herself simulated symptoms of botulism in the hope that the convulsions of strychnine poisoning would be confused with the paralysis and impeded breathing caused by the bacillus.

The defence tried to shift the blame to Frank Fenton, at least to suggest a conspiracy with Florence, but it was no use. The jury were out for only forty minutes. They pronounced her guilty, the judge sentenced her to death, and she was hanged just twenty-three days later, this being some twenty years before the institution of a Court of Appeal.

After the execution Frank and Ada Fenton emigrated to the United States and settled in New England. Fenton's reputation had gone before him. He was never again able to practise as a doctor but worked as the travelling representative of a firm of pharmaceutical manufacturers until his death in 1932. He never married. Ada, on the other hand, surprisingly enough, did. Ephraim Hurst fell in love with her in spite of her sickly constitution and withered leg. They were married in the summer of 1902 and by the spring of 1903 Ada Hurst was dead in child-birth.

By then Paraleash House had been re-named The Limes and lime trees planted to conceal its forbidding yet fascinating façade from the curious passer-by.

———◆———

The parcel from Carlyon Brent arrived in the morning with a very polite covering letter from Amyas Ireland, grateful in anticipation. Wexford had never before seen a book in this embryo stage. The script, a hundred thousand words long, was bound in red, and through a window in its cover appeared the provisional title and the author's name: *Poison at Paraleash, A Reappraisal of the Winchurch Case* by Kenneth Gandolph.

"Remember all that fuss about Gandolph?" Wexford said to Dora across the coffee pot. "About four years ago?"

"Somebody confessed a murder to him, didn't they?"

"Well, maybe. While a prison visitor, he spent some time talking to Paxton, the bank robber, in Wormwood Scrubs. Paxton died of cancer a few months later, and Gandolph then published an article in a newspaper in which he said that during the course of their conversations, Paxton had confessed to him that he was the perpetrator of the Conyngford murder in 1962. Paxton's widow protested, there was a heated correspondence, MPs wanting the libel laws extended to libelling the dead, Gandolph shouting about the power of truth. Finally, the by then retired Detective Superintendent Warren of Scotland Yard put an end to all further controversy by issuing a statement to the press. He said Paxton couldn't have killed James Conyngford because on the day of Conyngford's death in Brighton Warren's sergeant and a constable had had Paxton under constant surveillance in London. In other words, he was never out of their sight."

"Why would Gandolph invent such a thing, Reg?" said Dora.

"Perhaps he didn't. Paxton may have spun him all sorts of tales as a way of passing a boring afternoon. Who knows? On the other hand, Gandolph does rather set himself up as the elucidator of unsolved crimes. Years ago, I believe, he did find a satisfactory and quite reasonable solution to some murder in Scotland, and maybe it went to his head. Marshall, Groves, Folliott used to be his publishers. I wonder if they've refused this one because of the Paxton business, if it was offered to them and they turned it down?"

"But Mr. Ireland's people have taken it," Dora pointed out.

"Mm-hm. But they're not falling over themselves with enthusiasm, are they? They're scared. Ireland hasn't sent me this so that I can check up on the police procedural part. What do I know about police procedure in 1900? He's sent it to me in the hope that if Gandolph's been up to his old tricks I'll spot what they are."

The working day presented no opportunity for a look at *Poison at Paraleash,* but at eight o'clock that night Wexford opened it and read Gandolph's long introduction.

Gandolph began by saying that as a criminologist he had always been aware of the Winchurch case and of the doubt which many felt about Florence Winchurch's guilt. Therefore, when he was staying with friends in Boston, Massachusetts, some two years before and they spoke to him of an acquaintance of theirs who was the niece of one of the principals in the case, he had asked to be introduced to her. The niece was Ada Hurst's daughter, Lina, still Miss Hurst, seventy-four years old and suffering from a terminal illness.

Miss Hurst showed no particular interest in the events of March 1900. She had been brought up by her father and his second wife and had hardly known her uncle. All her mother's property had come into her possession, including the diary which Ada Fenton Hurst had kept for three years prior to Edward Winchurch's death. Lina Hurst told Gandolph she had kept the diary for sentimental reasons but that he might borrow it and after her death she would see that it passed to him.

Within weeks Lina Hurst did die and her stepbrother, who was her executor, had the diary sent to Gandolph. Gandolph had read it and had been enormously excited by certain entries because in his view they incriminated Frank Fenton and exonerated Florence Winchurch. Here Wexford turned back a few pages and noted the author's dedication: *In memory of Miss Lina Hurst, of Cambridge, Massachusetts, without whose help this reappraisal would have been impossible.*

More than this Wexford had no time to read that evening, but he returned to it on the following day. The diary, it appeared, was a five-year one. At the top of each page was the date, as it might be 1 April, and beneath that five spaces each headed 18 . . . There was room for the diarist to write perhaps forty or fifty words in each space, no more. On the 1 January page in the third heading down, the number of the year, the eight had been crossed out and a nine substituted, and so it went on for every subsequent entry until March 6, after which no more entries were made until the diarist resumed in December 1900, by which time she and her brother were in Boston.

Wexford proceeded to Gandolph's first chapters. The story he had to tell was substantially the same as Hallam Saul's, and it was not until he came to chapter five and the weeks preceding the crime that he began to concentrate on the character of Frank Fenton. Fenton, he suggested, wanted Mrs. Winchurch for the money and property she would inherit on her husband's death. Far from encouraging Florence to seek a divorce, he urged her never to let her husband suspect her preference for another man. Divorce would have left Florence penniless and homeless and have ruined his career. Fenton had known that it was only by making away with Winchurch and so arranging things that the death appeared natural, that he could have money, his profession and Florence.

There was only his word for it, said Gandolph, that he had spoken to Florence of botulism and had warned her against these particular canned herrings. Of course he had never seriously expected those cans to infect Winchurch, but that the fish should be eaten by him was necessary for his strategy. On the night before Winchurch's death, after dining with his sister at Paraleash House, he had introduced strychnine into the port decanter. He had also, Gandolph suggested, contrived to bring the conversation round to a discussion of food and to fish dishes. From that it would have been a short step to get Winchurch to admit how much he had enjoyed *Filets de hareng marinés à la Rosette* and to ask Florence to have them served again on the following day. Edward, apparently would have been highly likely to take his doctor's advice, even when in health, even on such a matter as what he should eat for the fourth course of his dinner, while Edward's wife did everything her lover, if not her husband, told her to do.

It was no surprise to Frank Fenton to be called out on the following evening to a man whose spasms only he would recognise as symptomatic of having swallowed strychnine. The arrival of Dr. Waterfield was an un-looked-for circumstance. Once Winchurch's symptoms had been defined as arising from strychnine poisoning there was nothing left for Fenton to do but shift the blame on to his mistress. Gandolph suggested that Fenton attributed the source of the strychnine to Anstruther's chemist's shop out of revenge on Anstruther for calling in Waterfield and thus frustrating his hopes.

And what grounds had Gandolph for believing all this? Certain entries in Ada Hurst's diary. Wexford read them slowly and carefully.

For 27 February 1900, she had written, filling the entire small space: *Very cold. Leg painful again today. FW sent round the carriage and had John drive me to Pomfret. Compton says rats in the cellars and the old stables. Dined at home with F who says rats carry leptospiral jaundice, must be got rid of.* 28 February: *Drove in FW's carriage to call on old Mrs. Paget. FW still here, having tea with F when I returned. I hope there is no harm in it. Dare I warn F?* 29 February: *F destroyed twenty rats with strychnine from his dispensary. What a relief!* 1 March: *Poor old Mrs. Paget passed away in the night. A merciful release. Compton complained about the rats again. Warmer this evening and raining.* There was no entry for 2 March. 3 March: *Annie gave notice, she is getting married. Shall be sorry to lose her. Would not go out in carriage for fear of leaving FW too much alone with F. To bed early as leg most painful. 4* March: *My birthday. 26 today and an old maid now, I think. FW drove over, brought me beautiful Indian shawl. She is always kind. Invited F and me to dinner tomorrow.* There was no entry for 5 March, and the last entry for nine months was the one for 6 March: *Dined last night at Paraleash House, six guests besides ourselves and the Ws. F left cigar case in the dining room, went back after seeing me home. I hope and pray there is no harm.*

Gandolph was evidently basing his case on the entries for 29 February and 6 March. In telling the court he had no strychnine in his dispensary, Fenton had lied. He had had an obvious opportunity for the introduction of strychnine into the decanter when he returned to Paraleash House in pursuit of his mislaid cigar case, and when he no doubt took care that he entered the dining room alone.

The next day Wexford re-read the chapters in which the new information was contained and he studied with concentration the section concerning the diary. But unless Gandolph were simply lying about the existence of the diary or of those two entries—things which he would hardly dare to do—there seemed no reason to differ from his inference. Florence was innocent, Frank Fenton the murderer of Edward Winchurch. But still Wexford wished Burden were there so that they might have one of their often acrimonious but always fruitful discussions. Somehow, with old Mike to argue against him and put up opposition, he felt things might have been better clarified.

And the morning brought news of Burden, if not the inspector himself, in the form of a postcard from Agios Nikolaios. The blue Aegean, a rocky escarpment, green pines. Who but Burden, as Wexford remarked to Dora, would send postcards while on his honeymoon? The post also brought a parcel from Carlyon Brent. It contained books, a selection from the publishing house's current list as a present for Wexford, and on the compliments slip accompanying them, a note from Amyas Ireland. *I shall be in Kingsmarkham with my people at the weekend. Can we meet? AI.* The books were the latest novel about Regency London by Camilla Barnet; *Put Money in Thy Purse*, the biography of Vassili Vandrian, the financier; the memoirs of Sofya Bolkinska, Bolshoi ballerina; an omnibus version of three novels of farming life by Giles de Coverley; the *Cosmos Book of Stars and Calendars*, and Vernon Trevor's short stories, *Raise me up, Samuel*. Wexford wondered if he would ever have time to read them, but he enjoyed looking at them, their handsome glossy jackets, and smelling the civilised, aromatic, slightly acrid print smell of them. At ten he phoned Amyas Ireland, thanked him for the present and said he had read *Poison at Paraleash.*

"We can talk about it?"

"Sure. I'll be at home all Saturday and Sunday."

"Let me take you and Mrs. Wexford out to dinner on Saturday night," said Ireland.

But Dora refused. She would be an embarrassment to both of them, she said, they would have their talk much better without her, and she would spend the evening at home having a shot at making a coil pot on her own. So Wexford went alone to meet Ireland in the bar of the Olive and Dove.

"I suppose," he said, accepting a glass of Moselle, "that we can dispense with the fiction that you wanted me to read this book to check on police methods and court procedure? Not to put too fine a point on it, you were apprehensive Gandolph might have been up to his old tricks again?"

"Oh, well now, come," said Ireland. He seemed thinner than ever. He looked about him, he looked at Wexford, made a face wrinking up nose and mouth. "Well, if you must put it like that—yes."

"There may not have been any tricks, though, may there? Paxton couldn't have murdered James Conyngford, but that doesn't mean he didn't tell Gandolph he did murder him. Certainly the people who give Gandolph information seem to die very conveniently soon afterwards. He picks on the dying, first Paxton, then Lina Hurst. I suppose you've seen this diary?"

"Oh, yes. We shall be using prints of the two relevant pages among the illustrations."

"No possibility of forgery?"

Ireland looked unhappy. "Ada Hurst wrote a very stylised hand, what's called a *ronde* hand, which she had obviously taught herself. It would be easy to forge. I can't submit it to handwriting experts, can I? I'm not a policeman. I'm just a poor publisher who very much wants to publish this reappraisal of the Winchurch case if it's genuine—and shun it like the plague if it's not."

"I think it's genuine." Wexford smiled at the slight lightening in Ireland's face. "I take it that it was usual for Ada Hurst to leave blanks as she did for March 2nd and March 5th?"

Ireland nodded. "Quite usual. Every month there'd have been half a dozen days on which she made no entries." A waiter came up to them with two large menus. "I'll have the *bouillabaisse* and the lamb *en croûte* and the *médaillon* potatoes and french beans."

"Consommé and then the parma ham," said Wexford austerely. When the waiter had gone he grinned at Ireland. "Pity they don't do *Filets de hareng marinés à la Rosette*. It might have provided us with the authentic atmosphere." He was silent for a moment, savouring the delicate tangy wine. "I'm assuming you've checked that 1900 genuinely was a Leap Year?"

"All first years of a century are."

Wexford thought about it. "Yes, of course, all years divisible by four are Leap Years."

"I must say it's a great relief to me you're so happy about it."

"I wouldn't quite say that," said Wexford.

They went into the dining room and were shown, at Ireland's request, to a sheltered corner table. A waiter brought a bottle of Château de Portets 1973. Wexford looked at the basket of rolls, croissants, little plump brioches, miniature wholemeal loaves, Italian sticks, swallowed his desire and refused with an abrupt shake of the head. Ireland took two croissants.

"What exactly do you mean?" he said.

"It strikes me as being odd," said the chief inspector, "that in the entry for February 29th Ada Hurst says that her brother destroyed twenty rats with strychnine, yet in the entry for March 1st that Compton, whom I take to be the gardener, is still complaining about the rats. Why wasn't he told how effective the strychnine had been? Hadn't he been taken into Fenton's confidence about the poisoning? Or was twenty only a very small percentage of the hordes of rats which infested the place?"

"Right. It is odd. What else?"

"I don't know why, on March 6th, she mentions Fenton's returning for the cigar case. It wasn't interesting and she was limited for space. She doesn't record the name of a single guest at the dinner party, doesn't say what any of the women wore, but she carefully notes that her brother

had left his cigar case in the Paraleash House dining room
and had to go back for it. Why does she?"

"Oh, surely because by now she's nervous whenever
Frank is alone with Florence."

"But he wouldn't have been alone with Florence, Winchurch would have been there."

They discussed the script throughout the meal, and
later pored over it, Ireland with his brandy, Wexford with
coffee. Dora had been wise not to come. But the outcome
was that the new facts were really new and sound and
that Carlyon Brent could safely publish the book in the
spring. Wexford got home to find Dora sitting with a
wobbly looking half-finished coil pot beside her and deep
in the *Cosmos Book of Stars and Calendars*.

"Reg, did you know that for the Greeks the year began
on Midsummer Day? And that the Chinese and Jewish
calendars have twelve months in some years and thirteen
in others?"

"I can't say I did."

"We avoid that, you see, by using the Gregorian Calendar and correct the error by making every fourth year a
Leap Year. You really must read this book, it's fascinating."

But Wexford's preference was for the Vassili Vandrian
and the farming trilogy, though with little time to read he
hadn't completed a single one of these works by the time
Burden returned on the following Monday week. Burden
had a fine even tan but for his nose which had peeled.

"Have a good time?" asked Wexford with automatic
politeness.

"What a question," said the inspector, "to ask a man
who has just come back from his honeymoon. Of course I
had a good time." He cautiously scratched his nose.
"What have you been up to?"

"Seeing something of your brother-in-law. He got me to read a manuscript."

"Ha!" said Burden. "I know what that was. He said something about it but he knew Gandolph'd get short shrift from me. A devious liar if ever there was one. It beats me what sort of satisfaction a man can get out of the kind of fame that comes from foisting on the public stories he *knows* aren't true. All that about Paxton was a pack of lies, and I've no doubt he bases this new version of the Winchurch case on another pack of lies. He's not interested in the truth. He's only interested in being known as the great criminologist and the man who shows the police up for fools."

"Come on, Mike, that's a bit sweeping. I told Ireland I thought it would be OK to go ahead and publish."

Burden's face wore an expression that was almost a caricature of sophisticated scathing knowingness. "Well, of course, I haven't seen it, I can't say. I'm basing my objection to Gandolph on the Paxton affair. Paxton never confessed to any murder and Gandolph knows it."

"You can't say that for sure."

Burden sat down. He tapped his fist lightly on the corner of the desk. "I *can* say. I knew Paxton, I knew him well."

"I didn't know that."

"No, it was years back, before I came here. In Eastbourne, it was, when Paxton was with the Garfield gang. In the force down there we knew it was useless ever trying to get Paxton to talk. He *never* talked. I don't mean he just didn't give away any info, I mean he didn't answer when you spoke to him. Various times we tried to interrogate him he just maintained this total silence. A mate of his told me he'd made it a rule not to talk to policemen or social workers or lawyers or any what you might call es-

tablishment people, and he never had. He talked to his
wife and his kids and his mates all right. But I remember
once he was in the dock at Lewes Assizes and the judge
addressed him. He just didn't answer—he wouldn't—and
the judge, it was old Clydesdale, sent him down for contempt. So don't tell me Paxton made any sort of confes-
sion to Kenneth Gandolph, not *Paxton*."

The effect of this was to reawaken all Wexford's former
doubts. He trusted Burden, he had a high opinion of his
opinion. He began to wish he had advised Ireland to have
tests made to determine the age of the ink used in the 29
February and 6 March entries, or to have the writing examined by a handwriting expert. Yet if Ada Hurst had
had a stylised hand self-taught in adulthood . . . What
good were handwriting experts anyway? Not much, in his
experience. And of course Ireland couldn't suggest to
Gandolph that the ink should be tested without offending
the man to such an extent that he would refuse publica-
tion of *Poison at Paraleash* to Carlyon Brent. But Wexford was suddenly certain that those entries were false
and that Gandolph had forged them. Very subtly and
cunningly he had forged them, having judged that the ad-
dition to the diary of just thirty-four words would alter
the whole balance of the Winchurch case and shift the
culpability from Florence to her lover.

Thirty-four words. Wexford had made a copy of the
diary entries and now he looked at them again. 29 February: *F destroyed twenty rats with strychnine from his
dispensary. What a relief!* 6 March: *F left cigar case in
the dining room, went back after seeing me home. I hope
and pray there is no harm.* There were no anachronisms—
men certainly used cigar cases in 1900—no divergence
from Ada's usual style. The word "twenty" was written in
letters instead of two figures. The writer, on 6 March, had

written not about that day but about the day before. Did that amount to anything? Wexford thought not, though he pondered on it for most of the day.

That evening he was well into the last chapter of *Put Money in Thy Purse* when the phone rang. It was Jenny Burden. Would he and Dora come to dinner on Saturday? Her parents would be there and her brother.

Wexford said Dora was out at her pottery class, but yes, they would love to, and had she had a nice time in Crete?

"How sweet of you to ask," said the bride. "No one else has. Thank you, we had a lovely time."

He had meant it when he said they would love to, but still he didn't feel very happy about meeting Amyas Ireland again. He had a notion that once the book was published some as yet unimagined Warren or Burden would turn up and denounce it, deride it, laugh at the glaring giveaway he and Ireland couldn't see. When he saw Ireland again he ought to say, don't do it, don't take the risk, publish and be damned can have another meaning than the popular one. But how to give such a warning with no sound reason for giving it, with nothing but one of those vague feelings, this time of foreboding, which had so assisted him yet run him into so much trouble in the past? No, there was nothing he could do. He sighed, finished his chapter and moved on to the farmer's fictionalised memoirs.

Afterwards Wexford was in the habit of saying that he got more reading done during that week than he had in years. Perhaps it had been a way of escape from fretful thought. But certainly he had passed a freakishly slack week, getting home most nights by six. He even read Miss Camilla Barnet's *The Golden Reticule,* and by Friday night there was nothing left but the *Cosmos Book of Stars and Calendars.*

———————

It was a large party, Mr. and Mrs. Ireland and their son, Burden's daughter Pat, Grace and her husband and, of course, the Burdens themselves. Jenny's face glowed with happiness and Aegean sunshine. She welcomed the Wexfords with kisses and brought them drinks served in their own wedding present to her.

The meeting with Amyas Ireland wasn't the embarrassment Wexford had feared it would be—had feared, that is, up till a few minutes before he and Dora had left home. And now he knew that he couldn't contain himself till after dinner, till the morning, or perhaps worse than that—a phone call on Monday morning. He asked his hostess if she would think him very rude if he spoke to her brother alone for five minutes.

She laughed. "Not rude at all. I think you must have got the world's most wonderful idea for a crime novel and Ammy's going to publish it. But I don't know where to put you unless it's the kitchen. And you," she said to her brother, "are not to eat anything, mind."

"I couldn't wait," Wexford said as they found themselves stowed away into the kitchen where every surface was necessarily loaded with the constituents of dinner for ten people. "I only found out this evening at the last minute before we were due to come out."

"It's something about the Winchurch book?"

Wexford said eagerly, "It's not too late, is it? I was worried I might be too late."

"Good God, no. We hadn't planned to start printing before the autumn." Ireland, who had seemed about to disobey his sister and help himself to a macaroon from a silver dish, suddenly lost his appetite. "This is serious?"

"Wait till you hear. I was waiting for my wife to finish dressing." He grinned. "You should make it a rule to read your own books, you know. That's what I was doing, reading one of those books you sent me and that's where I found it. You won't be able to publish *Poison at Paraleash*." The smile went and he looked almost fierce. "I've no hesitation in saying Kenneth Gandolph is a forger and a cheat and you'd be advised to have nothing to do with him in future."

Ireland's eyes narrowed. "Better know it now than later. What did he do and how do you know?"

From his jacket pocket Wexford took the copy he had made of the diary entries. "I can't prove that the last entry, the one for March 6th that says, *F left cigar case in the dining room, went back after seeing me home,* I can't prove that's forged, I only think it is. What I know for certain is a forgery is the entry for February 29th."

"Isn't that the one about strychnine?"

"*F destroyed twenty rats with strychnine from his dispensary. What a relief!*"

"How do you know it's forged?"

"Because the day itself didn't occur," said Wexford. "In 1900 there was no February 29th, it wasn't a Leap Year."

"Oh, yes, it was. We've been through all that before." Ireland sounded both relieved and impatient. "All years divisible by four are Leap Years. All century years are divisible by four and 1900 was a century year. 1897 was the year she began the diary, following 1896 which was a Leap Year. Needless to say, there was no February 29th in 1897, 1898 or 1899 so there must have been one in 1900."

"It wasn't a Leap Year," said Wexford. "Didn't I tell

you I found this out through that book of yours, the *Cosmos Book of Stars and Calendars?* There's a lot of useful information in there, and one of the bits of information is about how Pope Gregory composed a new civil calendar to correct the errors of the Julian Calendar. One of his rulings was that every fourth year should be a Leap Year except in certain cases . . ."

Ireland interrupted him. "I don't believe it!" he said in the voice of someone who knows he believes every word.

Wexford shrugged. He went on, "Century years were not to be Leap Years unless they were divisible not by four but by four hundred. Therefore, 1600 would have been a Leap Year if the Gregorian Calendar had by then been adopted, and 2000 will be a Leap Year, but 1800 was not and 1900 was not. So in 1900 there was no February 29th and Ada Hurst left the space on that page blank for the very good reason that the day following February 28th was March 1st. Unluckily for him, Gandolph, like you and me and most people, knew nothing of this as otherwise he would surely have inserted his strychnine entry into the blank space of March 2nd and his forgery might never have been discovered."

Ireland slowly shook his head at man's ingenuity and perhaps his chicanery. "I'm very grateful to you. We should have looked fools, shouldn't we?"

"I'm glad Florence wasn't hanged in error," Wexford said as they went back to join the others. "Her marriage didn't begin with dearly beloved, but if she was afraid at the end it can't have been with any amazement."